T0383980

RULES
FOR
CAMOUFLAGE

RULES
FOR
CAMOUFLAGE

Kirstin Cronn-Mills

LITTLE, BROWN AND COMPANY

New York   Boston

Copyright © 2024 by Kirstin Cronn-Mills
Illustrations on chapter openers and page 318 copyright © 2024 by Kimberly Glyder
Illustrations on pages 319–22 copyright © 2024 by E. Eero Johnson

Cover art copyright © 2024 by Kimberly Glyder. Cover design by Gabrielle Chang.
Cover copyright © 2024 by Hachette Book Group, Inc.
Interior design by Carla Weise.

Illustration on title page © Black Creator 24/Shutterstock.com
Cover reference image for people © Ljupco Smokovski/Shutterstock.com;
for octopus © Yellow Cat/Shutterstock.com

Little, Brown and Company
Hachette Book Group
1290 Avenue of the Americas, New York, NY 10104
Visit us at LBYR.com

First Edition: June 2024

Little, Brown and Company is a division of Hachette Book Group, Inc. The Little, Brown name and logo are trademarks of Hachette Book Group, Inc.

The publisher is not responsible for websites (or their content) that are not owned by the publisher.

Little, Brown and Company books may be purchased in bulk for business, educational, or promotional use. For information, please contact your local bookseller or the Hachette Book Group Special Markets Department at special.markets@hbgusa.com.

Library of Congress Cataloging-in-Publication Data

Names: Cronn-Mills, Kirstin, 1968– author.
Title: Rules for camouflage / Kirstin Cronn-Mills.
Description: First edition. | New York : Little, Brown and Company, 2024. |
    Audience: Ages 14 and up. | Summary: During her senior year of high school,
    neurodivergent Evvie navigates school, friendships, and her first love.
Identifiers: LCCN 2023021726 | ISBN 9780316567954 (hardcover) |
    ISBN 9780316567992 (ebook)
Subjects: CYAC: Neurodiversity—Fiction. | High schools—Fiction. |
    Schools—Fiction. | Interpersonal relations—Fiction. | LCGFT: Novels.
Classification: LCC PZ7.C88149 Ru 2024 | DDC [Fic]—dc23
LC record available at https://lccn.loc.gov/2023021726

ISBNs: 978-0-316-56795-4 (hardcover), 978-0-316-56799-2 (ebook)

Printed in the United States of America

LSC-C

Printing 2, 2024

THIS ONE'S FOR YOU, MY SWEET DOLLYFACE.
YOU'RE AWESOME. NEVER FORGET.

1

WE'RE HERE.

We're weird.**

We don't need to be fixed.

**We can use this word if we want. You don't get to use it against us.

Though I know you will anyway.

2

THERE'S A CEPHALOPOD ON MRS. DEARBORN'S HEAD.

She has no idea.

The octopus—is it my octopus? I don't think so—perches on her salt-and-pepper hair like a hat, its mantle draping down the back of Dearborn's head. The octo has one arm on each of Dearborn's shoulders, one arm around each of her ears, two arms cuddled around her chin, and two arms circled around her eyes. Poor baby is agitated; I know because it's flashing different colors as Dearborn talks. The arms around her chin move down to her throat. Dearborn has no idea how strong that octopus is, and I'm not gonna mention it.

"EVVIE!"

My eyes fly open.

"Yes?" I try to act like I've not just been dreaming in the middle of Biology, but it's pretty impossible when I'm also trying not to fall off my stool.

Laughter everywhere.

In my defense, it's not even 10:00 a.m.

"Please wake up." She glares, no octo glasses in sight. "And we need to talk after class, all right?" She raises her eyebrows as the class snickers around me.

I don't say anything. I just try to remember what she looked like with an octopus for a hat.

Lucky for me, she goes back to lecturing about the nervous system. The human nervous system. I sit up straight, blink my eyes really, really hard, and log in to Kahoot when she tells me to.

Finally, class is over. The sophomores file out of the room, nudging each other and probably talking about me, the only senior. I glare at them. Mrs. Dearborn fiddles with the stuff on her desk until the room is empty except for us.

"Let's discuss your presentation, shall we?" She's gearing up for the bad news. I can see it in her face.

"It's Friday, Mrs. Dearborn. Please don't do this right now." And I book it out the door.

I don't look back. I don't go to my next class. I head straight for the Lair.

Lockers. Doors. Hallways.

Then I have to look back. Maybe she's not following me.

Of course she is.

Mrs. Dearborn's fussy, annoying face is locked into her *I'm just trying to help you, Evvie, just trying to help you see the right way* expression. The one she wears when I've done something that doesn't match her rigid and careful explanation of the world. The one I've seen since I was twelve, when she was my middle school principal.

I'm not supposed to run, and she can't, because she must be over sixty, nor would she dare, because teachers don't run in school unless someone's on fire, so I walk super fast. The distance between us expands.

Fridays are always a bit chaotic, and Mrs. Dearborn gets stuck talking to Mr. Garfield, our principal, who comes out of the office right as she goes by. He's oblivious to the fact that she's chasing-but-not-chasing me.

When she's finally looking him full in the face, I risk it and pull my key from my pocket, then unlock the Lair and slide inside. I'm sure she sees me go in.

I let my breath out in a whoosh.

Some squishy, beat-to-hell furniture is to my left, a small couch and two armchairs, and there's a window behind the couch. Why there's a window in a band storage room is beyond me. It looks onto the school's lawn, the bench by the sidewalk, and the street that goes by our stupid school in our tiny little punk-ass town.

It's sunny right now. Spring can be decent in Minnesota. Two thousand Bluestem Lake residents are having regular days out there, not being chased by stressful teachers, and not caring two shits what I do for my presentation.

The Lair is maybe twelve feet wide and thirty feet long, with two rows of big cupboards to my right. They cover the walls, on the top and bottom. Directly in front of me is a door that leads into the band room. On that door is a sign that says KEEP OUT.

Above that door, in squiggly, cheerleader-y purple and black letters on a big piece of poster paper, it says THE LAIR.

Vaguely band-ish noises are floating under the door.

A defining feature of this space: pieces of paper taped everywhere. It looks like a ream of paper exploded.

Gus Gus is in one of the armchairs. He looks up at me, then at his book.

KNOCK KNOCK KNOCK. With feeling.

"Evvie! I saw you go in there!" So polite and nice.

The door handle twists once, twice.

KNOCK KNOCK KNOCK. With intensity.

"Evvie!" Not as polite and nice.

I hear the band-room noises stop midnote. There's a brief pause, then the door to the band room opens. Ms. Brownlee—she lets us call her Rachel—comes into the Lair, smiles at me, and motions me down toward the end of the room where we have our reset pods—unused instrument cupboards with pillows, blankets, and good smells—great for naps or panic attacks. I climb in one and shut the door.

FWOOSH. I imagine Rachel composing her face into its best teacher look, camouflage perfectly arranged.

Random fact: did you know octopuses are better at camouflaging themselves than chameleons? They're the best in the animal kingdom. FWOOSH.

Rachel's determined footsteps move to the door, and I hear her turn the handle. "May I help you, Mrs. Dearborn?"

There's a polite but annoyed huff from the hallway. "I saw Evvie Chambers go through this door, which she seems to have locked behind her. It's not supposed to be locked during the school day, Ms. Brownlee. You know that."

"I didn't realize the problem, Mrs. Dearborn. Thank you for pointing it out." I hear Rachel's keys jingle as she unlocks the door.

"But if I could—"

"If I see Evvie, I'll let her know you're looking for her.

If you could be so kind as to move your foot?" No answer from Mrs. Dearborn. "Have a good morning." The door closes before Mrs. Dearborn has anything else to say.

I hear Gus Gus chuckle.

"Evelyn?" Rachel knocks gently on the door of the cupboard.

I crack the door and peer up at her. "Yes?" Our reset pods are all in the bottom row of cupboards.

She's got her teacher face on, but it's fading. There's a smile there, too. The Lair was her creation, long before I got to high school, for all the kids who need time-outs on a regular basis. Good time-outs. Not the punishing kind. "Mrs. Dearborn giving you a hard time?"

"She wants to tell me I can't use octopuses for my final project." I emerge, stand up, and crack my back.

Her smile is steady and comforting. "If you're all right, I need to get back to lessons. Carry on." And she walks out of the instrument room, back to the kids in the band room.

Rachel says she created the Lair because she wanted one when she was in high school. Her brain is also unruly. She grew up here, went to college, and came back to teach, which I think is uncalled for. Rachel knows Mrs. Dearborn's bullshit—as a student and as a teacher. Dearborn's been here for a million years.

The music-ish sounds resume.

On the wall above the window, above the squishy furniture, there are four pieces of paper. They've been there since I've been coming in here, so I don't know how old they are. We take turns recoloring them when they get faded. The pieces of paper are laid out like a banner, and each has a different word on it. Each letter has wild colors and patterns. The words say:

HOP OFF MY WANG

Because nobody ever, ever does.

Gus Gus watches me walk over to the door, open it slightly, and use my key to undo what Rachel had done. He doesn't make eye contact.

"Mrs. Dearborn is not your fan."

"She is if you ask her. She thinks she can help me be a better student and has all the right plans to make it work." I flump on the couch.

"She is not interested in cephalopods."

"Nope. Just foxes. Gotta follow the assignment rules. Only mammals for your final presentation."

Gus Gus is a senior, like I am, and he's on his way to MIT. He's quiet, but he's always paying attention, unless he's lost in a favorite topic. He doesn't say much, but when he does, it's either smart or entertaining. We've known each other since kindergarten, like most of us at this backward school, and he's my brain cousin, because our official labels have a few overlaps. In this tiny-ass town, it's surprising he's not my actual cousin. He's also one of my favorite people.

He's reading *A Brief History of Time* by Stephen Hawking, and he puts his finger in the book to hold his place. "Sorry you didn't get Mackowski for the makeup class. Aretha is an amazing animal."

"She is." Seniors don't normally take Biology, but I'm not exactly a normal senior. Aretha is the octopus at the Minnesota Zoo, and she is my most favorite creature on Earth aside from my cat, Popcorn.

He goes back to reading. I look at my phone to see how much time I have until next period. Twenty-seven minutes.

I study Gus Gus, who's cool as a cucumber. "Who are you hiding from?"

He keeps reading. "Nobody. Not a fan of people. As you may know. Plus, I have three study halls in a row, because I'm done with all my classes except for choir. I have a lot of free time." He tunes me out for Hawking. Fair enough.

I close my eyes and contemplate what to do next.

I need Dearborn to see how cool octopuses are.

I need to make it through the semester. And graduate.

I need to disappear into thin air.

I wish I had a way to get Aretha to my school, Bluestem Lake Area High School, also known as BLAHS—did

no one check the acronym? The district itself is BLAS—
Bluestem Lake Area Schools—and I don't know if that's
better or worse than BLAHS. It's forty miles, give or
take, between the zoo and BLAHS. If Dearborn could
meet Aretha, she'd see how amazing Aretha is and why
Aretha should be the subject of a final presentation.

I have no physical, mental, moral, spiritual, or educational authority to make anything happen.

Octopuses are the closest thing to space aliens on
Earth, if there aren't actual aliens among us. If I have my
way, I'm writing a ten-minute presentation on them so I
can pass my biology class. The one I should have passed
when I was a sophomore, but I didn't, because I missed
most of the year. Though not on purpose.

While I was gone, I bonded with octopuses, and we've
stayed bonded for more than two years.

Mrs. Dearborn has assigned me to present about
foxes. I like foxes fine. But they are not octopuses. She's
frustrated, not mad, Evvie, just frustrated! with me for
objecting. Aretha is an invertebrate cephalopod, not a
vertebrate mammal.

Mrs. Dearborn will not hop off my wang.

The door opens again, and Rose slips in, key in hand.
She looks at me and Gus Gus. "Pods empty?"

I gesture. "All for you."

She climbs in.

"Anything we can do?"

She shakes her head. And the door shuts. I hear her spray the lavender calming mist.

The band students start practicing "The Star-Spangled Banner." Ouch. Our band is grades seven through twelve, because we're a small school. Seventh graders don't know the song yet.

Gus Gus starts humming under his breath, still reading Hawking. His hand flutters in time to the song.

I close my eyes and sit for another fifteen minutes. Then I rummage through the snack boxes until I find a CLIF Bar and start to choke it down.

Meds + school day = no appetite. But you gotta fuel up.

FILM DIVA: EVVIEEEEEEEEEEEE.

It's my best friend, Ken—normally I don't get a text from her between morning and lunch. She used to go to BLAHS, but then she moved to Apple Valley, so she lives closer to Aretha than I do—the Minnesota Zoo is in her town. Our text streak is years long—back to middle school, when we got our first phones. At the moment, she's Film Diva in my phone, because she wants to make movies. I'm <3 <3 <3 in hers—octopuses have three hearts.

Ken used to tell people her name was Kendra or Kennedy if they were giving her shit about having a boy name, but now she doesn't care. She cared a lot when we were kids. Now she knows it's just another thing that makes her a badass.

She's that friend you always went trick-or-treating with when you were in elementary school. The one you laughed with when someone farted in eighth-grade gym. The one you learned to drive with in the church parking lot by her house, while your moms screamed, one in the front seat and one in the back, and her dad waved his arms like a Muppet in front of the car, trying to keep you away from the cones he set up. The one you cried with for three days when her flaky, weird parents got a wild hair up their ass to move away the summer before your senior year. That friend.

> **FILM DIVA:** less than two months,
> Evvie! LESS THAN TWO MONTHS. i'm
> gonna explode.

Apple Valley West graduates before BLAHS, so she's got an advantage.

> **<3 <3 <3:** i'm gonna explode from
> the bullshit that is Mrs. Dearborn.

Ken knows Dearborn, too. She was a model student—always polite to teachers and administrators. Dearborn loved her. Ken would sneak me granola bars when I had to sit in the office after school.

FILM DIVA: soon you can disappear
from that school FOREVER.

> **<3 <3 <3:** Dearborn may kill me
> before that.

FILM DIVA: got that short film i made
about composting into a student film
festival this summer. super cool! here's
the link!

> **<3 <3 <3:** very super cool!

Ken's new school is three times the size of BLAHS. She'd never admit it, since she's still pissed at her parents, but Apple Valley West has been great for her because they have a photography and film club. We're way too small for that. Ken's on her way to be a film major at DePaul in Chicago. She wants to make documentaries.

How the hell does a person know what they want to do in life? Overwhelming. Life is a long time. How could a person want to do the same thing for all of it?

Next year for me = gap year. Working at the zoo. And that's all I need to know right now.

I finish the last bite of my CLIF Bar. Blech.

Ken never came to the Lair when she lived here—it's not really for her, but she was still welcome. She never believed me when I said it was her loss. She has new friends at AVW—like a football field full of them, judging from her Insta. When she was here, she was kind of a loner, like me.

I find it super weird she made a film about composting, but who am I to say what's weird?

I miss her.

The bell rings. The pod pops open, and Rose crawls out. She looks at me, and out the door she goes—FWOOSH—camouflage up. Kids like us are easy targets. FWOOSH. Mine goes up, too, as I follow her into the hall. Gus Gus keeps reading. He's our anchor.

Now we're back in the wild, away from our Lair. Now we're fair game again, if someone sees through our protection.

Rose goes to Math, I think. I go to Psychology.

In my head, I hear the video Gus Gus made for his media class last fall, about the benefits of neurodivergence. I want to walk around with that video on an iPad, holding it out in front of me. Gus Gus made his voice really deep, Mufasa-deep, and started the video with, "We are your scientists. Your Olympic gold medalists. Your kids next door. Your teachers, bankers, and doctors. We discovered relativity. We program your computers, write your music, invent machines, and make sculptures. Our unique brains are genetically adapted to push humanity forward. Neurotypical people, you need us. So stop being such assholes."

He actually said that. In a school assignment.

Gus never camouflages. Ever.

Do you know how many people want Lair kids to be "normal," as in, like them? So, so many. Because it's easier. *Difference is disruptive and causes chaos.* That is literally something Mrs. Dearborn said to me.

Guess what we're not? And that's fine.

We're Albert Einstein, Simone Biles, Michael Phelps, Emma Watson, and the mind of fucking Bill Gates, and who's more powerful than Bill Gates? My brain is more like Bill Gates's than Mrs. Dearborn's.

You know who's really good at camouflage? Sir Anthony Hopkins, the actor. His brain disguises him so well that he's morphed himself into six different Academy Award–nominated characters, with two wins, one for that scary motherbeeper Hannibal Lecter. Camouflaging like an octopus, sly like a fox, he is.

Foxes are just a symbol of Dearborn's desire to force me into her box.

Fox boxes.

Box of foxes.

Whatever.

How does she know I'm not a genius, too?

3

WHEN I WAS LITTLE, I ADORED MY BABYSITTER, JORDAN. SHE LIVED NEXT DOOR and played Barbies and trucks without complaining, plus she'd jump rope with me—jumping rope is super old-school, but it gave me a place to put my bouncing around. She'd listen to my secrets about boys I thought were cute, the times I stole my mom's bite-size Snickers, and how I wanted a Great Dane, because they were so big.

One day, when I was supposed to be doing my summer reading, I heard her tell her mom her brain was tired from listening to me, and her ears were going to fall off her head. She said I never shut up. Her mom laughed. But I was crushed.

I quit talking to her, and to most people, really. She

didn't understand what had happened—and my mom didn't, either. I just looked at them. Jordan stopped babysitting not long after that, and her family moved away a couple months later. I was glad. Every time I looked out the window and saw her, I got a knot in my stomach.

Then, in middle school, we had an English teacher named Mrs. Johnson—Minnesota, land of ten thousand Johnsons, which is also hilarious because "johnson" is slang for penis—but we called her Mrs. Buddha. She was always teaching us about slowing down and peacing out, as in literally slowing down and cultivating peace, not vacating the premises. *Your mind can be tamed,* she'd say, *so make it do what you want.* I rolled my eyes so hard, they almost fell out. BUT. Mrs. Buddha taught us how to make lists and outlines, which she called arguments. She told us over and over that lists and arguments would serve us well when we were adults. Our brains would be more organized and less chaotic.

Mrs. Buddha's lists gave me a place to put all those words Jordan shamed me for.

Now I have piles of journals in my room, full of lists and arguments. Arguments and lists tacked to my wall. In my school notebooks. They also help me rehearse, if I have to say something exactly right.

Once I met Aretha, I started making lists and arguments in multiples of eight. Of course.

Patterns are soothing, so I'm very exact—1, a, i, on and on.

I need to send Mrs. Buddha some flowers.

WHY DEARBORN WILL NOT HOP OFF MY WANG

1. She thinks she knows me.
   a. She knew my middle school self.
   b. I was relatively untamed in middle school (exhausting but fun AF).
2. She thinks it's her job to improve me. Because there's something wrong with me.
   a. Ha. There's no improving perfection.
   b. But seriously—fuck off with that. I need ideas for *adapting*, not *improving*.
   c. She told me *brains have specifications for efficiency,* and I should work toward them.
   d. There's no such thing. I checked.
3. When she was the middle school principal, I was in her office a lot, but there were three significant moments.
   a. The time I used my phone to film a teacher hitting a sleeping girl on the head with a book—that was big.

i. She was homeless and her family was living in their car, but the teacher either didn't know or care.

  ii. He didn't get in trouble.

b. The time I sassed off to our gym teacher and said she needed to think more about kids who don't like gym class—also big, because the teacher yelled and told me I was a bleeding-heart liberal.

  i. That teacher didn't get in trouble, either—for yelling or for assuming my political stance.

c. Then there was the time I yelled directly at Dearborn, for patronizing me.

  i. She was trying to get me to calm down, because Vandal McDaniel, who happens to be her great-nephew, was picking on a girl named Farisa and saying her homemade lunch smelled bad.

  ii. I was not interested in calming down.

  iii. Talking down to me makes me furious.

       iv. It's also highly counterproductive.

       v. Vandal McDaniel is still an asshole. To this day.

4. She thinks she's really kind and she can teach me kindness skills.

   a. I am totally kind, just not to her.

   b. She is incredibly unkind to students who aren't like her.

   c. She thinks Vandal is kind, which proves her idiocy.

5. She thinks she's a savior of all the *troubled* (her word) kids.

   a. Not a troubled kid.

   b. Don't need saving.

6. She doesn't like the way I think—I need to *come back to reality, please.*

   a. Whose reality?

7. She doesn't believe neurodivergence is an explanation for anything.

   a. She also doesn't believe in medication or accommodations.

   b. She says we're not trying hard enough. WTF.

   c. *The stakes are so high, Evvie! So much is riding on your high school career!*

      i. Nah.

     d. *I don't trust flexible systems and rules.*
         i. What a shame. They're really quite helpful.
     e. Everyone should do things exactly like her.
     f. Isn't that what everyone wants?
     g. To be happy and successful like she is?
         i. She genuinely asked/told me this once, with a serious face.
         ii. We all naturally admire her precision and exactness!
         iii. What. The. Fuck.
8. She knows I see through her bullshit.
     a. I think she also knows I'm not afraid of her.
     b. I think that bothers her.
     c. So. What.

I hear my mom banging pots together in the kitchen, and I look at my phone: 9:52 a.m. I hope she fed the kitty. I hope she'll make me some scrambled eggs.

No texts from Ken. Even when she's been out, she's up by eight—she's a biological weirdo. I always wake up to a text from her.

<3 <3 <3: where are you, Film Diva?

We haven't seen each other for at least a month. Saturdays are for lying in bed, thinking about things. Like the fact that I'm almost done with high school. And the Minnesota Zoo is gonna be my hangout—like, my full-time space—for an entire year. Me and Aretha are going to plot a takeover.

WHY OCTOPUSES ARE FREAKING COOL
1. They adapt to their environment.
2. They remain badass and completely themselves, no matter what.
3. They have no pretense.
4. They use tools and they play. Only smart animals do those things.
5. They escape through the smallest spaces and squirt water at people they don't like.
6. Their blood is BLUE.
7. They are never on anyone's wang. Ever.
8. They don't care about you.
   a. Though they seem to like and/or respect their caregivers.
   b. Whether we can establish friendships with them is still a matter of scientific debate.

I hear a SKREEEEEEEEEEE noise on my door, which is Popcorn dragging her claws down the plywood. Cats don't believe in closed doors. She's all white with some faint yellow spots randomly scattered around, like the hulls on kernels of popcorn.

I get up, open the door for the cat, and go pee. When I come back, Popcorn's tucked into the spot where I was, blinking up at me like, *thanks for warming up my space*. I get back into bed and cover us up. She purrs immediately.

> **<3 <3 <3:** can we meet up today?
> get a coffee in Savage?

It's Saturday. Why not get a coffee with your bestie?

Forty miles isn't exactly far away. But it's far sometimes, when Ken works and I volunteer, and there's homework, and she's got a raging social life.

Popcorn's a giant lump under the covers, cuddled next to my knee.

It's starting to smell like breakfast.

Aretha's probably eating shrimp for breakfast.

WHY OCTOPUSES ARE SIGNIFICANT IN MY LIFE
1. I have deep feelings for them.
   a. I love them immensely.
   b. I respect and admire their skills.

c. I still have a healthy fear of them.

d. They change color when they sleep. As they dream.

   i. I wish I could do this.

e. Their camouflage game is always on point.

   i. In some videos, you literally cannot tell what is a rock and what is an octopus arm.

f. When they need to escape danger, they SWIM BACKWARD SUPER FAST.

g. Let me repeat: BACKWARD.

2. They live in a scary place and don't mind.

a. The ocean is scary as shit, with so many scary things in it.

b. It's so big.

c. With so much power.

d. Humans are aliens there.

e. Octopuses are aliens in our world.

3. I found octopuses when I needed them.

a. I wanted their creativity and problem-solving abilities.

b. Plus their badass-ness and their camouflage.

c. I needed to know it was okay to be me.

    d. Guess how many octopus videos I
       watched on YouTube when I was
       out of school?
       i. Maybe five thousand.
       ii. Maybe ten thousand.

4. When I was a sophomore, I went on fall break
   and didn't go back.
   a. I couldn't get out of bed.
   b. I couldn't slow my brain down.
   c. I couldn't concentrate.
   d. I couldn't tell anyone what the
      fuck was going on, because I didn't
      know myself.
   e. I was scared.
   f. Ken was petrified and had no idea
      what to do.

5. My mom thought I was faking my anxiety.
   a. I was not.
   b. My mom was more petrified than
      Ken, but she didn't tell me.
   c. I feel horrible about that.

6. They tried having a "homebound teacher"
   come to me.
   a. I wouldn't do the work.
   b. My brain wouldn't shut up.
   c. I couldn't explain the whirl in my head.

    d. Or why I couldn't let people look
       at me.

7. I could not go to school.

    a. Literally.

    b. Could.

    c. Not.

8. We tried exposure therapy for my anxiety.

    a. I couldn't even make it into the
       parking lot of the school.

    b. I would crawl onto the floor of
       the car.

    c. I couldn't look at the building.

    d. Every day, I'd cry.

9. My mom cried as much as I did, though she
rarely let me see it.

    a. I'll be sorry about that for the rest
       of my life.

10. I tried a project-based school—where you
incorporate science, math, and English into a
giant project—instead of BLAHS.

    a. Everything was still going too fast
       in my head.

    b. I couldn't make choices about what
       to do.

    c. But I also got suspended before I
       had to quit.

     i. I brought cigarettes on the
        school bus.

     ii. I showed them to a kindergarten kid.

     iii. Whoops.

11.   I tried an online school.

    a. I never logged on.

    b. I stayed in my room, in a blanket,
       and watched Netflix.

12.   I was home from October to the end of the
school year.

    a. That's not pandemic-long, but it's
       long enough.

    b. That's a long freaking time for a
       mom to worry.

13.   Then it was summer, and my sophomore year
was a complete bust.

    a. Then we both cried.

    b. Popcorn tried to cheer us up by
       bringing us her catnip mice.

14.   I begged my mom to have me tested, to get the
whirl in my head to stop.

    a. She did.

    b. We figured it out, though it took a while.

    c. The solutions aren't perfect, but
       they work.

    d. Mostly.

15. When I came back to BLAHS, I was both a
    junior and a sophomore.
    a. One kid came up to me and said,
       I thought you died.
    b. I said, *I did.*
    c. Which is kind of true.
    d. Ken was my protector that year.
16. Now I'm a person who understands my brain.
    a. I can work with it.
    b. Usually.
    c. And that knowledge is priceless.

And now I have octopuses.

It was a shitty, shitty year.

My mom got diagnosed about sixteen months later. She
said it explained her entire life—the good parts and the
terrible decisions, too. She hugged me and told me how
grateful she was that we could share this ugly, wacky,
marvelous brain. Then she cried and apologized over and
over for not figuring it out sooner—for me or her.

She thinks she's a terrible mom.

I think she's the best mom in the world. She loves me
and understands me. That's huge.

Also, Rachel understands me.

The other kids in the Lair understand me.
Ken gets me, too.
Dearborn has no clue.

FILM DIVA: can't hang out today, gotta
work. remember?

> **<3 <3 <3:** no—sorry—whoops.

FILM DIVA: did you watch the
composting vid?

> **<3 <3 <3:** not yet!

FILM DIVA: *eye roll*

> **<3 <3 <3:** i'll watch! promise.

FILM DIVA: blah blah blah. love you,
dumbass. maybe next weekend.

> **<3 <3 <3:** love u 2, diva. come to
> the zoo sometime when i'm there?

FILM DIVA: smart. text me your sked.

"You and kitty hungry for some breakfast?" My mom
is in the bedroom doorway. Her name is Josie, and she
looks like a regular Saturday-morning mom: sweats and
a T-shirt, hair a mess, in the business of getting shit done.

"Can we have scrambled eggs, and maybe some pancakes?"

"Probably. But only if you help me do house chores."

"That's a fair trade."

"I'll put a tiny piece of bacon in Popcorn's dish." She motions at me with the spatula. "Take your sheets off and put them in the wash."

I stretch. "Hop off my wang, huh?"

"Not a chance. I'm your mom." She goes back to the kitchen.

"I tried, kitty." I get up, pull the covers back over Popcorn, and go get some food.

4

JUDGING FROM OUR WALLS AND THE DOORS TO THE INSTRUMENT CUPBOARDS, Mrs. Buddha's teachings have rubbed off in the same way for most folks who visit the Lair. There are lists and arguments EVERYWHERE—and Rachel keeps bringing us paper and markers. Each list has bunches of different handwriting on it since the Lair is so old.

According to Rachel, the first year the Lair existed, she didn't tell anyone except a couple teachers. She asked them to look out for kids who seemed like they could use a break. A few kids showed up one day. Then they told a couple more. Then they started making lists and arguments, decorating the walls, and making the reset pods. By the time I got here last year, it was pretty perfect. Even middle school kids will sneak in sometimes, if they can make it to our side of the building without being seen. More kids know about it than teachers, I'm guessing, but that's the way it should be. Grown-ups can kiss our collective ass. Except for Rachel, of course.

When I'm feeling stressed before school, I come in and read a few pages. People who agree with an entry on a list add stars for emphasis.

Nobody in here does the lists in eights. Too bad for them.

On the first cabinet door:

THINGS WE FIND GROOVY
Adventures (six stars)
Silence (seven stars)
Screwing around (fifteen stars)
Earbuds (ten stars)
Sunrises and sunsets (two stars)
Nature (two stars)
Baboons (six stars)
Books (nine stars)
Reset pods (five stars)
*Old-timey rap groups, like Public Enemy and
   NWA* (eleven stars)

This list goes on for three and a half cabinet doors. Each sheet is taped under the next one, so the page bottom sticks out, sort of like stairsteps, at the bottom of the door. When a door is covered, the list moves to the next door.

After that list is done, there's another set of pages on doors:

THINGS WE DO NOT FIND GROOVY

Man buns, tho bonus points for bucking gender stereotypes (two stars, along with a note that says "I feel personally attacked")

Selfishness (twenty stars)

MAGA HATS (with a note that says "for Ahmed," and another note in someone else's handwriting that says "for all of us!") (seven VERY BIG stars)

Getting up (twenty-five stars)

Having to get gas in my car—why doesn't it last forever? (six stars)

School—not built for galaxy brains! (twenty stars)

Lima beans (six stars)

Helping grown-ups clean the house (seventeen stars)

The idea that we're all just shouting into the void, and that when we die, there's literally... NOTHING (this one has six stars and a note that says "Wow, Brett, way to harsh my mellow.")

This list goes on for seven cabinet doors. Obviously people are more crabby than they are optimistic.

Before I was diagnosed, I'd heard rumors there was a peace-out spot for escaping AND being peaceful, in school, but I thought they were just rumors. Then a kid in an online support group—a dude from Chanhassen, not Bluestem Lake—was raving about it, because he knew someone who'd graduated from BLAHS. I hated that online support group, but it made me investigate. I walked around the entire building one day after school until I figured out which two doors it might be behind. The next day, I knocked on the first one, and nobody answered. I knocked on this one, and Gus Gus was there.

There's one list that's even longer than the not-groovy list: ten doors of it, plus pieces tacked up on various empty wall spaces. In big letters on the top, it says *WHY I LIKE YOU*. Rachel says she started it the day the Lair had its first visitors.

The most recent list has these ideas on it:

> *you don't wear boring shoes*
> *you listen to IRON MAIDEN!*
> *you understand that spiders are not bugs, they're*
>   *SPIDERS*
> *you like me in return*

you understand my stutter is related to
   brain variation, not intelligence—YOU ROCK
   JOE BIDEN, FUCK YEAH STUTTERERS,
   I SEE YOU.
you understand I'm more than my label
you brought me kettle corn before school
you smiled at me when Ms. Wright was yelling
   at me for forgetting my homework
you bought me some milk when I forgot my
   lunch PIN
your smile lights up the room

At the bottom of each page, in Rachel's handwriting, it always says *BECAUSE YOU'RE YOU*, in green marker, with Rachel's signature smiley face.

These lists make me believe the world is better than it really is.

Tuesday. I have Biology at 8:55. It's the first official period of the day, after boring old homeroom that starts at eight thirty, where we do nothing but listen to announcements, finish homework, maybe chat with people, and look at our phones. My homeroom teacher is Mrs. Shapiro, and she's nice, even when I'm the last person out the door every day. Mrs. Dearborn's room is a hall away, not very far, but getting myself there is about as easy as getting to the moon without a spaceship. Or getting to the bottom of the Grand Canyon without a donkey.

Every day, I say "Don't make me do this" when I walk out the door. And Mrs. Shapiro, who's known me since I was a freshman, pats my arm and says, "You'll be fine." I say, "Ha." Every day, this is our ritual. She knows I disappeared sophomore year. She knows I just want to be done.

Not long, and I'm free to forget every single thing that's happened in this building. Not long, and sophomore year washes away in the tides of time.

I get to Dearborn's room and slip onto the stool at the back table in the lab. The bell rings, and Dearborn starts to call roll. I'm five names down.

"Evelyn Chambers?"

I raise my hand, as we're required. She looks up, grimaces, and nods. "Stay after class today, or else." She follows it up with a weak smile.

Or else? Can a teacher really say that?

People keep raising their hands to say they're here, but her comment causes a new round of folks to turn and look at me. I didn't get a lot of stares after Octoberish, because by then everyone had noticed there was a senior in the class. But every so often, she'll say something to point me out, like today. And the stares start again.

I am nobody's spectacle.

I look at the floor and pretend not to care.

Dearborn goes on with her lecture for the day: the integumentary system, also known as skin. She's got cool videos, and she gets out the clickers to test our knowledge. Big whoop. We're a little school but with good tech! We have up-to-date classrooms!

When we do our presentations, we have to address all the systems of our subject's body: nervous, endocrine, respiratory, digestive, muscular, integumentary, skeletal, immune, renal, reproductive, hematopoietic, and circulatory. Lucky for me, octopuses have all of these things, too—mostly, sort of. Enough that I can punt. Plus, they have REALLY, REALLY COOL intelligence. That's the thing that gets me. They think about what they want to do—they don't just act on instinct. They're generally solitary and territorial, and then you throw in their camouflage abilities . . . my mind is off on octopuses again.

"Evelyn!"

Shit.

FWOOSH.

I try to compose my face so it looks like I was paying attention. "Yes?"

"Why aren't you clicking? Don't you know the six functions of skin?" Dearborn is two seconds away from tapping her foot at me.

I clicked most of them, I swear I did. "Protection, absorption, excretion..."

"Please get your head out of the clouds and come back to us." She frowns and glares.

"...secretion, regulation, sensation! I know them!"

"Please don't shout at me after I've moved on." Another glare. But she hadn't moved on. She hadn't said another word.

I look at the floor. Look at the floor. Look at the floor.

Everyone goes back to clicking. I read the slides and remember what she says. But if she even swings her head my direction, I look at the floor.

When the bell rings, I consider ditching school and going home. Then I consider skipping my next class and heading for the reset pods. I will myself to walk to the front of the room and stand by her desk.

"Thank you for staying, Evelyn." Her voice is always silky smooth when she's got some sort of punch to deliver. I've heard it all year.

All the sophomores look at me as they file out.

When the room is quiet, she shuts the door so the next class will stay outside for thirty seconds. Our passing period is only three minutes long, so she's gotta make it quick, but she's doing everything for dramatic effect.

She touches my arm. "Evelyn."

"Yes?" I'm looking at the top of the wall behind her, willing the tears away. I cry when I'm mad.

"I've given careful consideration to your request to do octopuses instead of foxes for your final presentation, and I don't think I can allow it. No one else in the class is allowed to do an invertebrate."

"No one else is a senior." I say it to the flag above her head, to the posters of Charles Darwin and Jane Goodall.

"That's true, but that doesn't make you special. I know you have special needs, but you have to obey the rules, just like everyone else. The school is being generous by allowing you to be here with the sophomores. Learning how to work within given parameters is an important skill for the adult world, including college." She smiles with her mouth but not her eyes. "Remember, the stakes are high. Colleges care about your high school career."

I look at the ceiling. "The school's legally obligated to make me take this class, but why do we have to do vertebrates? Is that a legal requirement, too?" I risk a look at her face.

A beat. Her eyes blink fast. "We do vertebrates

because I say we do vertebrates, and you'll have to do foxes. Our goal is to get you on to the real world. This is how we'll do it." She pats my arm again. "Now scoot quick before you're late for your next class." She says this like it's my fault I'll be late.

I bolt out the door and head to the art room, trying to walk as fast as I can so nobody will see me cry. When I get there, Mx. Thompson, who we call T, can see on my face that I've had a bad morning already. T is their superhero name.

"Need a moment, Evvie? I'll get your work out for you."

"Yes, please." T is a brand-new teacher, but they're cooler than almost anyone in the school. They're out and proud and started a gender and sexuality alliance the first semester they were here—the Crusaders, "fighting for justice, equity, and good snacks at school!" It says so on their bulletin board. T has progress flags in strategic places around the room.

"Under the table you go, then." They point, and I go. "Come back when you're ready." It's peaceful under there, and they brought rugs for us to sit on.

"Right." I settle myself in a spot and say my mantras in my head with my eyes closed. *Nobody defines me but me. I am proud to be me. I'm a capable, worthy human being.*

People who don't think so can hop off my wang. I am a cool and interesting octopus. Those aren't really my mantras, but I figure they're useful. My real mantra is *Fuck off, you stupid-ass world, and leave me the fuck alone.*

Today I am not proud to be me. But if I say the positive ones enough times, they might come true.

Sometimes T comes through the Lair because they use Rachel's office as a reset pod. They know the score about brains and their bullshit.

Why should high school be high-stakes? What are "stakes"?

I think I know, but I look it up on my phone, just in case. Consequences. If something's high-stakes, it has big consequences if it gets screwed up.

I call bullshit. High school is just what you wade through to get to the next thing.

Maybe I don't understand. I could definitely be stupid here.

But I'm betting it's Dearborn.

After school, I get in my car and head to the zoo. It's an Aretha day, thank god. By the time I get to the zoo, which takes maybe forty-five minutes, longer if the traffic is bad, I've calmed down. Now I can focus on the tasks ahead, which are feeding and enriching Aretha. And washing crap, because volunteers have to do the crap work. But whatever. Aretha. Feeding and enriching Aretha.

That's what they call playing with her—enrichment. It's mostly just offering her various toys, puzzles, and games, and watching her burn through them. Sarah, the big-boss head aquarium keeper, told me she's never seen such a smart octopus, and Lucie, the assistant keeper, agreed with her.

Aretha is a day octopus, and she came to the Minnesota Zoo right around the time the aquarium staff was spinning a lot of Aretha Franklin in the back rooms of the complex. She's not that big—three pounds, maybe, and her arms are maybe each three feet long. Day octopuses are also known as big blue octopuses, since their Latin name is *Octopus cyanea*. They are extraordinarily good camouflagers and hunt during the day—they're crepuscular and diurnal, because they're mostly active in the twilights of early morning and dusk, crepuscular, and those times still count as daytime, making them diurnal; please enjoy two nerdy science terms. They have their dens in coral reefs in shallowish tropical waters and don't live very long, which I try not to think about, because there's no real way to tell how old an octopus is. I can't bear to think about Aretha dying. I hope she's no more than three or four months old.

Aretha came to us from another zoo, so she's never been wild, but Lucie, her main keeper, studied wild day octopuses at a place called the Maui Ocean Center. She told me the Maui Ocean Center's octopuses never die in captivity—divers find them in the wild, keep them for just a few months to study them and let others admire them, and then release them so the octopuses can live out the rest of their years on Earth as free creatures. This is beautiful and poetic.

Aretha wasn't the first octopus I met. When I started volunteering—my mom was desperately trying to find something for me to do during my sophomore year, and the zoo needed help—they had a male day octopus named Bernard, after Bernie Sanders, who is also uber-smart like an octopus. He wasn't very social, so he didn't bond much with us. Then our boy Bernard died of old age, and Aretha came. That's when I fell permanently in love.

Aretha is still a little bit scary to me—she's unpredictable, demanding, and otherworldly. But she's the only other creature I've met on this planet who seems to think in thirty dimensions at once. She'd fit right into the Lair.

Octopus fact: our last common ancestor was a wormy thing, and it lived probably seven hundred fifty million— MILLION—years ago.

Next year, I'll be paid to care for Aretha. Sarah said she'll hire me the week I graduate.

As I get my zoo badge out of my glove compartment, I can feel my blood pressure drop. Nobody here knows I failed a year of school. And I get to cuddle with Aretha today. All is well.

It didn't cross my mind until I started volunteering that aquariums have backstage areas—DUH—where zoo workers take care of the animals and tanks. The one at the Minnesota Zoo is giant, like the size of a small gym, with different levels of access for different aquarium tanks at different heights in the zoo exhibits. There are stairs and platforms everywhere, so workers can access the tanks from above and behind. It's kind of like a play structure. We also have spaces around the room—on the floor, of course—for sinks, tables, cupboards, and storage areas, plus industrial refrigerators for the animals' food.

The Tropical Reef, where Aretha hangs out, is huge—like the height of a two-story wall. Her backstage access is off to the side, and her hidey-hole—a huge conch shell—is in the bottom of it. That's where she goes if she doesn't want to be out doing reef business, or if she doesn't want to talk with us. She's got a fence of other small shells set up around her conch shell. Octopuses decorate.

Sarah isn't there, but Lucie is, and she motions me to

Aretha's part of the tank. "We started enrichment early today." She points.

I look, and Aretha is very busy solving a puzzle of three boxes. She has to get the first box open to get the second box open to get the third box open. Inside the third box is a shrimp, and Aretha loves shrimp.

We watch. It takes about fifteen minutes for her to get it done. After she gets the shrimp out, she passes it along her suckers and into her beak, which is underneath where her arms begin. Then she stares at us like, *Okay, what's up for my next shrimp?*

I put one on my palm and put my hand in the water. She extends her arm and takes it from me with all the delicacy of a society lady picking out the nicest pastry on the tray. It disappears up her arm of suckers.

Lucie hands me more shrimp, and we repeat the process. Then I put my arm in the tank, with an empty hand, and Aretha explores it, looking for more food. When she doesn't find any, she inks at me and retreats, skidding under some rocks. I laugh.

Lucie does, too. "Obviously she's unhappy with this turn of events." She hands me a jar with a shrimp in it— a simple baby-food jar, with a really easy lid. "Give her this."

I put it in the water and watch it float. Aretha peeks

out from behind her rocks. BOOM. An arm snatches the jar, and another arm gets the lid off, and the shrimp is gone.

Maybe it took ninety seconds.

We finish feeding Aretha by giving her the most difficult toy we have—she has to get a shrimp out of a box in a maze, and she has to move the box through the maze to make it happen. It takes her about forty minutes, but she gets it. While she puzzles it out, I scrub tanks and chop chum and do all the things Lucie tells me to do—a lot of mindless, messy work, but I can wear my earbuds—and then, when I'm done, Lucie says I can do Aretha's version of cuddling, which means I put my arms in the tank and wait. Aretha moves right over, engulfs my arms with four of hers, and tangles us together like we're besties, because we are. Me and my undersea girlie are tight.

She encircles my hand with those four arms, feeling me like she's done every time. Maybe she's tasting me. Or smelling me. I don't know. As she's doing that, I realize I forgot to take off my bracelets. Aretha, however, has not missed this fact, and she works one off my wrist. I watch it slowly sink to the bottom of her tank.

"Aretha stole my bracelet." It's the first time she's done something like this.

Lucie laughs. "You might get it back and you might not."

"It was just a string one. She can have it."

Lucie waves her hand at our cuddling session, like she's blessing it. "We'll see what she does with it."

Aretha's got her arms about halfway up mine, which is both scary and awesome. Holding hands with an octopus is unlike anything else in this world. Her suckers are STRONG. I can still feel their pull when they're off my skin—it tingles.

Aretha inquires but doesn't judge what she finds. She evaluates and accepts, or rejects, but it's never personal. She can't be anything but herself: smart, intense, never boring or the same twice.

Another thing about octopuses: you are definitely not in charge when you're interacting with them. *They're* considering *you*, rather than the other way around. They are always, always the boss, and you're damn lucky if they accept you into their world.

Lucie comes over to coo at her—she talks to Aretha like she's a kitten or a puppy. "How's my tiny sea goddess today? Are you my sweet sugar girl?" She puts her arm in the tank, and Aretha slides two of her arms over to Lucie, but she doesn't let go of me. We become a glorious octo cuddle puddle.

Lucie lets Aretha move her fingers around, arms twining and sliding through them. "Have you gotten your teacher to okay your octopus project?" She's in grad school at the University of Minnesota, and she might be in her late twenties. She still remembers bad high school teachers.

"Nope. Foxes. She was very emphatic." I focus on letting Aretha feel my arms, and Aretha starts being a smart-ass. She tries to pull me into the tank, and I have to disengage, carefully but firmly. She reaches back to me with one arm, then with another, she picks up my bracelet and hands it back—well, her version of handing it. I put it back on, and Aretha takes it off again. Then she starts tugging hard on me. I laugh.

"Aretha." Lucie wags her finger at the tank—using the hand and arm that Aretha isn't curled around. "You can't keep Evvie, no matter how much Evvie loves you."

I pull my arm out gently and carefully. It's red from Aretha's suckers. "I'm sure foxes are cool and all, but they do not compare to this beauty."

Lucie takes her arm out, too, and hands me a towel. "Invertebrates for the win."

Aretha squirts water at us and jets to her hidey-shell.

I sponge off my arm. "I know, sweetheart. But I've got to go. I'll be back, I promise." I give the towel back to

Lucie. "I'll find a way to share Aretha. She's too amazing to keep to ourselves."

Lucie nods. "Let me do some asking around. There may still be an octopus report in your future." Then she looks back down in the tank at Aretha. "You're not getting any more arms to chew on today, madam."

Aretha's come back out of her shell and is looking straight up, straight at Lucie. You can tell she's thinking, *I'm all alone down here, and I do not appreciate it.*

"Gotta go, Lucie. Good luck with that paper." She's got a big one coming up. Invertebrates and how to keep them happy in zoos.

She rolls her eyes. "Yeah, right. Grad school is a lot of work for maybe not much return. But thanks."

"My mom says that, too." I give her a wave, blow Aretha a kiss, and head out of the aquarium prep area. Walking through the halls, I try not to trip over the old folks who are going suuuuuuuuuuuuuuuper slow in the hallway. Today is senior day, and the aquarium is a big draw for the silver set.

If I get old enough to become one of the silver set, I'm not going to be walking slow in the hallways. I'm gonna be back with the animals, volunteering. Even when I have to walk with a walker, my brain will still be a hundred miles in front of me.

Right before I make it out of the aquarium building, I see Hugh, who I call Blue. He's busy feeding the manta rays.

Want to know how to embarrass the shit out of yourself? When someone tells you their name is Hugh, and you say, *You mean like a shade of a color, that kind of hue? Great to meet you, Blue.* I should have crawled into a hole after that.

Luckily, he laughed. Then he one-upped me in nerdery and told me about the pelagic zone, also known as ocean water that never touches either land or the ocean floor, full of big fish that travel miles and miles, kind of like an ocean within an ocean. Ocean currents travel around it, rather than through it, which is why the water never touches land, *so if you want to call me Blue, that's fine, because I love the ocean, and it's blue, especially the pelagic part.* Not what you expect to learn the first time you meet someone, but Blue's not your average fish nerd. We've been friends since that day a year ago.

"Hey, Blue."

He's way too cute and way too normal for me—with the exception of his fish-nerd skills, of course. We text at least once a week, sometimes on weekends, just about regular life stuff, or school, or zoo stuff. Very casual. No depth.

I've wanted to ask him out but haven't had the guts.

Blue looks up and gives me a big smile when he hears me.

"Hey, Evvie. Pretty sure I'm kind of orange today. Want to feed a ray before you go?" He holds up a bucket of shrimp, so I grab some. Mantas cruise around in the ocean with their mouths open, eating tiny things we almost can't see, but in captivity, they eat shrimp that aren't that small. Right after I slide a few morsels in, a stingray comes winging by, silent and graceful.

Blue's humming under his breath, looking hard at the rays, like he's concentrating on something I can't see or hear.

"You okay, dude?"

He jerks his head to face me, like I've caught him doing something he shouldn't. "Oh! Yeah. Fine. Just fine." I see the blush creep up his neck. "Just thinking too much."

"Been there, done that."

"Not quite like this." The blush moves all the way up to the tips of his ears. "School's almost over, thank god." Blue goes to school in Minnetonka, and he's a senior, too.

"Did you go to prom?" He texted me that his prom was last weekend.

"Oh, hell no." He smiles. "Who wants to spend money on all that stuff?" He smiles again, and I notice how very cute that smile is. "Did you know there's a prom-ish thing here in a few weeks?"

"I saw." I nod at the big poster that's on the wall not far from the rays. It says ZOO PROM: WHERE EVERYTHING'S WILD! Underneath that, it says FOR PEOPLE WHO LIKE ZOOS. Underneath that, in much smaller letters, it says FOR PEOPLE WHO DIDN'T FIT IN AT THEIR OWN PROM, AND/OR ANY OTHER ANIMAL OR FISH NERDS. Obviously the marketing department has a sense of humor. It's for any age—kids to grown-ups—and it's a fundraiser for the zoo. You're supposed to dress up and drink punch and boogie down to whatever silly band they have.

Blue smiles at me. "If a person's going to dress up and dance, better to do it with fellow zoo nerds instead of assholes who don't think I'm cool enough to sit at their lunch table."

"You're cute enough to sit at my table anytime." Then I realize what I've said and try to look less alarmed than I really am.

Blue's not frowning, though, and he's not laughing in my face. He's just smiling.

So I smile back.

We're awkward.

"You'd really want to go with me? You'd look nice in a dress." His face goes scarlet again and he closes his eyes. "I should not have said that."

I can feel my face is just as scarlet as his, but I laugh. "I don't even own a dress."

He leans down and pets the rays floating close to the surface. They like him and his attention. "They asked me to volunteer at it. Maybe you could, too?"

"Sure. If I get my damn Aretha report done, that is." I check the date again. "I'm trying not to do it last minute."

Blue looks at me. "Your Aretha report?"

"Long story. I'm supposed to write about foxes, but I'm writing about Aretha. My teacher will just have to accept it."

Right? If the goal is to get me out of high school, and my report is quality, Dearborn will have to pass me. If it's exactly what she wants, just with Aretha, she can't say no.

Right?

"How is she today?"

"Who?" My brain is yanked back to the ray pool.

"Your sea goddess Aretha." Blue can see I was absent for a moment.

"We cuddled. She sassed us."

He grins and digs out more shrimp to throw in the ray pool so the rays have to go find them. They slide away when they feel the shrimp hit the water. "Aretha is a thousand times more interesting than foxes, so obviously your teacher is dumb." The blush has faded a bit, but it comes right back when he looks at me. "You'd really go? Volunteer on a Saturday night?"

"You think I'm hanging out anyplace special on Saturday nights?" I hold his eyes with mine, and it's the most curious, unusual feeling I've ever had.

I've never not been myself with him. And maybe that's okay.

His grin is big. "Okay. That's good." He flings what's left in his shrimp bucket into the ray pool, and I see the rays glide after the splashes.

"Well. I gotta go." I gesture at the door. "Gotta work on that report."

"Yeah." He's still smiling. "I'll text you."

"Perfect. Have a good night." I smile in return.

"You too." He keeps smiling. We both smile. It's awkward.

He felt that connection, too. I know he did.

My spatial awareness fails me, so I don't realize how close the outside door is, or how many steps I take backward, and I make a giant THUD into the glass, rather than turning and exiting gracefully. Two oldsters walking by look around to see where the weird noise came from.

"Gotta open it first." Blue grins and mimes opening a door.

The glass is still vibrating, as is my elbow. "Right.

Long day. Too many octopus thoughts." I roll my eyes, give him a wave, and get out of there as fast as I can.

When I get home, my mom is asleep with her head on the books that are open in front of her on the table. Sleeping is rare for her, so I leave her be. Popcorn rubs past my legs, meowing and telling me she's not been fed, which I know is fake news. But I give her a couple of princess pebbles anyway.

I heat up the oven for a frozen pizza while I think about Blue. And Aretha. And foxes. And dresses and dancing. And whether I can accomplish that much of a glow-up.

And how much I want to do something rude to Dearborn.

She thinks she's so NICE. She JUST WANTS THE BEST FOR ME.

HA. Really what she wants is to control me. And squish my originality.

She's pretty much the whole world, represented by one person.

Thinking about Dearborn makes me white-hot angry. So I stand still and breathe for a bit, then go back to improving my dopamine: I eat my pizza and pet Popcorn.

Will Dearborn accept an octopus report?

I look up a few fox facts on my phone. Boring.

She'll have to accept what she gets. And she's getting Aretha.

When I go to bed, Popcorn at my feet, I think some more about Blue.

Where do I get a dress to wear to a zoo prom?

> **<3 <3 <3:** where does a person get a fancy dress?

FILM DIVA: you're not a fancy dress person, you're Evvie! 😆😆😆😆😆😆

> **<3 <3 <3:** obviously you're not doing homework?

FILM DIVA: just quietly drinking in my room on a Tuesday. as you do.

> **<3 <3 <3:** mmmmmmm...maybe go to bed?

FILM DIVA: soon. gotta finish this.

Then there's a photo of three single-shot bottles of Pink Whitney, her vodka of choice. Two are empty, and one has some missing.

> **<3 <3 <3:** girl. it's a school night.

FILM DIVA: hush. i know. i'll teach you
about fancy dresses later. love u.

<3 <3 <3: love u too.

Have I mentioned I'm worried about Ken? She didn't
do this when she lived in Bluestem Lake. She drank like
a regular teenager—when she could, and not that often.
But the last six months, you'd think she was old enough
to buy for herself.

I know I need to see Ken more—I *want* to see her
more. But drunk people freak me out. Too unpredictable. Ken can get a mean mouth.

I pet Popcorn some more. And send angry thoughts
at Ken's parents, for making her move.

5

"Evvie, do you know where my keys are?" She comes into the living room, where I'm on the couch with my computer.

"Right by the front door." I point at the floor, and she follows my finger. "They slipped off the table." We both try very hard to put our keys in the same place every day.

She bends down to grab them, then comes over to kiss me on the forehead. "Thanks, my love. Hyperfocus on something useful."

"Same to you." I one-arm hug her, then she's out the door. No FWOOSH when she leaves. She doesn't need her camouflage when she works with her group.

Mom's a grad student at the University of Minnesota, studying adaptable and experiential education, specifically with a focus on people like us and the Lair kids. Her grad school peeps get together on Thursday nights to go over the data they've collected for their thesis projects. They're all supposed to graduate in August. Mom's hoping she can find a job in a school district around here.

During the day, she's a paraprofessional at the elementary school in town, for little people with confusing brains. Then she comes home to feed me and work on her thesis. She works all the time, but that's because she doesn't need much sleep. I sleep all the time. Mom says that's because I'm growing. I think it's because I've had enough of the world's bullshit.

When I walked in after school, my mom was slamming pots and pans around the kitchen. When I asked what was wrong, she said, "You can't fucking make lentil soup if you keep forgetting to put lentils on the grocery list!" Then she flopped onto a kitchen chair and closed her eyes. I went to the freezer and found some stew she'd made a few weeks ago. I heated it up. Nobody starved.

Our house is messy and cozy—sometimes too small—but it's not a pigsty. Sometimes things get pretty sketchy before one of us says, *Oh damn, better get the Ajax,* but isn't that true for everyone? Don't people have better things to do than monitor their cleanliness?

Little people don't notice when my mom forgets things. But big people do. Nobody understands when a grown-up can't grown-up very well. All adults must have the work ethic and stamina of a Clydesdale, and you'd better be able to do it all at the same time—*work, parent, sweep the goddamn floor.* I heard her say that to her grad school buddies. You'd also better keep your emotions together—who cares if you have smaller amygdalae or that your frontal lobe doesn't work so well? Shape up, worthless human. According to other Midwestern adults, that is. Midwesterners want everyone to WORK HARD, BEHAVE PROPERLY, and BE ON TIME, all the time, every time. Or there's something wrong with you.

I'm also going to make a terrible grown-up.

Mom says my dad left her because he couldn't understand why she didn't keep the house cleaner. And she talked too much. And she was lazy.

What the hell does he know?

My dad and I don't talk. He left when I was two and lives in California. He's never tried to visit, and I've never gone there. He sends money to my mom, and she puts it in an account for when I'm in college. That's it.

I honestly don't know how to feel about him—except blank.

I don't miss him, because I don't remember him, and I have no idea who he is. People want me to be sad about not having a dad, but I don't know what it's like to have one. Nobody believes me when I say I don't take his lack of contact personally, but why worry about it? My mom's all the parent I need, and he could be an axe murderer, or someone who eats octopus appetizers at fancy restaurants. She says he's a loan officer at a bank.

Forgetting is a part of this brain. Out of sight, out of mind. That's how it is with my dad.

Maybe someday I'll go see him. And maybe not.

Of course my mom feels bad about his absence, and also the stuff she thinks she's either doing wrong or not doing at all. I tell her not to worry, but she doesn't listen. Of course not.

It's almost dark outside. I don't turn on any lamps. I can see everything I need to.

Popcorn is curled up at the opposite end of the couch. She stretches out so I'll pet her tummy, and meows once. She's sick of hearing about Dearborn and octopuses.

Octopuses "talk back" to their keepers. One researcher watched an octopus stuff a stale squid down a drain while making eye contact with the researcher. *Fresh food only, please.*

Octopuses have blue blood because their oxygen is carried on hemocyanin, which has copper in it. The hemocyanin is how they stay warm when the water's colder.

Three-hearted octopuses are the opposite of heartless teachers.

Octopuses camouflage so well because of skin cells called chromatophores. When their brain (which brain? I don't know) signals those cells, the octopus can change the color or the texture of their skin. The mimic octopus can morph itself to match the shape of other animals to fool its prey. FWOOSH.

Humans, on the other hand, camouflage to cover our awkwardness, our obsessions, our unusual skills, and often our deep desire to be anywhere but a place where others are looking at us. We have to become experts at blending in, at not calling attention to ourselves. Octopuses don't camouflage out of embarrassment or shame—only to find food or stay safe.

Clearly, both humans and cephalopods know about the safety move.

No camouflage required in the Lair. We can be our sweet cephalopod selves. Outside the door? Better show up as a girl who likes boys, with cute hair and painted fingernails. Better show up as a guy who loves girls, football, cars, and sports statistics, in that order.

Otherwise, other ocean dwellers will eat you.

My phone vibrates. It's the one who camouflages with pink vodka.

FILM DIVA: still working on your octopus thing?

      <3 <3 <3: procrastination is my
      friend #4EVA

FILM DIVA: here's a video of an octopus
looking weird.

She sends a video of the mimic octopus morphing into a flatfish, a sea snake, and a poisonous lionfish—the vid with seven and a half million views.

      <3 <3 <3: thank you!

I don't want to tell her how many times I've seen it.

FILM DIVA: check out this short clip i
made for school about littering.

      <3 <3 <3: i'll watch it!

FILM DIVA: you better.

      <3 <3 <3: litter is wack. love you.

FILM DIVA: don't forget!

      <3 <3 <3: promise. random q: do
      you think high school is high-stakes?

FILM DIVA: ?? maybe? I suppose GPA could be? why?

        <3 <3 <3: Dearborn said it was. still thinking about it.

FILM DIVA: high-stakes is forgetting to feed Aretha. or Popcorn. or forgetting to take BC pills.

        <3 <3 <3: don't have those stakes, thank god. 😆😆😆✍

FILM DIVA: i should give it up. ✍ watch the video! gotta go! love you!

I watch her composting clip, the one I should have watched when she sent it. It's good. And funny. There's a dancing orange peel. The litter one is also funny, but this time there's a dancing taco wrapper.

        <3 <3 <3: the clips are good— littering and composting! dancing objects are hilarious.

FILM DIVA: cuz i'm good at film, u kno.

        <3 <3 <3: i do know.

I put the mimic octo video clip on one page of the PowerPoint. It looks very forlorn.

Procrastination is the ramp-up to the work. It always is.

But it sucks.

Forgetting your birth control pill is way more high-stakes than high school.

When my mom comes home, she wakes me up so I can go to bed. Once I finally fall asleep again, Dearborn is chasing me and I can't get the key in the door of the Lair. I wake up just as her hand clamps onto my shoulder.

For a second, I feel the tip of Aretha's arm on my face, touching me to say, *It's okay, Evvie. I'm here.* Then I realize it's just Popcorn's wet nose. She sniffs my face, I give her some pets, and she settles down in my armpit.

Popcorn is my girl. She's my own personal sun, she's so warm.

Aretha is also my girl, though she is not warm.

6

SAM IS A LAIR REGULAR, AND SAM KNOWS HOW TO PLAY THE FLUTE, THOUGH he quit band in eighth grade. Lately he's been on a Lizzo kick, and he taught himself the flute parts to both "Juice" and "About Damn Time"—thank you, YouTube. For a while, he was here at least five times a day, and he'd play both songs over and over. Rachel finally asked him to play each song one time per session, with no more than two flute performances per day. It was getting in the way of band because students could hear him.

Sam is your basic joy machine, so he flutes it out with gusto within Rachel's limits. Even though our ears ring from how loud—and sometimes sharp—he is, we still appreciate his gladness.

Today, Sam is fluting away during lunch and I'm reading. Then the door slams open and Rose falls in from the hall, with Sagal in tow. They both look like they've been running, and Sagal is crying. Not an average Tuesday thing to see.

"Sit. Sit." I jump up and point at the couch where I was. Sam stops playing.

Sagal sits, and Rose sits next to her. Both of them are fussing with Sagal's hijab, which I notice is almost off her head. I can see her hair, and I'm glad she's in a place where there are just four of us. Being the understanding human he is, Sam stands up and walks to the far end of the Lair, carefully not looking at Sagal. He turns his back to us and begins playing Lizzo again.

"What the hell happened?" I search for the box of Kleenex.

Rose keeps her arm around Sagal and reaches out her hand for the tissues. "Vandal McDaniel is a certified asshole."

"Absolutely."

"Is Vandal his real name?" Rose hands the box to Sagal without letting go of her.

"Legend goes his mom came from Idaho, where there's a college sports team called the Vandals."

"He tried to pull off Sagal's hijab. And Dearborn watched him do it."

"She didn't say anything?"

"No." Rose squeezes Sagal's shoulders. Sagal's trying to blow her nose and rearrange her hijab at the same time.

Vandal walks around BLAHS like he owns it. His dad's a fifth-generation Minnesota farmer, so Vandal will be the sixth, and he loves to brag about that fact. He's rich—so he brags about all the farming technology nobody else can afford—and he thinks he's funny. He also looks like a model, which is disgusting but true. Everything he wears is from Hollister or someplace like that.

He takes what he wants. And evidently, today he wanted a hijab.

What's even more gross is that he's supersmart, so he's top of our class and one of our graduation speakers. Most grown-ups think he's a good guy. Obviously he's stepped up his asshole game if he's yanking hijabs. But nobody will do anything. Besides Dearborn being his great-aunt, our lovely Principal Garfield is friends with Vandal's dad—they're old drinking buddies from their time at BLAHS. It feels like a safe bet that Vandal's dad would yank hijabs, too, if he was a teenage dude now.

"Asshole!" Sagal is still trying to tuck her hair in. She wrenches away from Rose and stands up, then paces around looking for a mirror. "Fucking asshole!"

I don't know much about Sagal, but the swears

surprise me. She tries to find her reflection in the window. "All I can see are the goddamn trees!" She's breathing hard and still crying, like she's just run a mile from a monster, which I suppose she has.

Sam stops playing. "Use the camera on your phone." He's still facing away from us. His flute starts again.

"God, we're dumb." I dig out my phone and hand it to Sagal.

Finally, she's satisfied with how it looks, and she flumps onto the couch to rest her re-hijabed head, closing her eyes with a big sigh. "What time is it?"

I check my phone. "Twelve fifty-nine." Bell rings in seven minutes.

She doesn't say anything. She just keeps her eyes closed.

My anger at Vandal—and at Dearborn—is exponential. But I make sure the fury doesn't take over my brain, because then we'd have a recently assaulted girl and a rage-machine girl.

Rose walks over to touch Sam on the shoulder as he's playing "About Damn Time," since he ran through "Juice" already. "You can come back to the couch."

He doesn't stop playing, just walks over and stands by the door. He looks at Sagal, then me, then Rose, appraising the situation.

"Thanks for the music, dude." I nod at him.

He nods, then stops at the end of the part and smiles.

"'I was born like this, don't even gotta try'"—which of course are lyrics from "Juice." He cocks his hip out for emphasis.

"We love you for it."

"Bet." Sam laughs and starts packing up his flute.

Sagal smiles, with her eyes still closed. "You a big Lizzo fan, Sam?"

"I'm a fan of Sasha Flute." He tucks his flute into an instrument cupboard and slips out the door. FWOOSH.

The bell rings. Sagal's eyes open, and she stands up. "Can I come in here more often?"

Rose and I look at each other, eyebrows raised. Nobody's ever asked that before—nobody with a normal brain, anyway. Weirdos have passed info about the Lair forever. But normal people don't come here.

"Um…sure? I guess?" I look at Rose to see if she agrees, and I can tell she's not sure, but she nods a little. "But you gotta keep it pure. This is a place for nerds, weirdos, oddballs, and outsiders."

Sagal nods. "Like a girl in a hijab at this school isn't those things?" I see Rose relax. Sagal slides out the door.

I look at Rose. "I think she'll be all right."

Rose gives me a glare. "If she's not, it's up to you to kick her out."

"Kick who out? Do we really kick people out of the Lair?" Rachel comes in the door just in time to hear Rose's words.

Rose crosses her arms. "Sagal."

Rachel smiles. "Sagal is fine. She wants to be a math professor. She's just as nerdy as the rest of you."

Rose drills Rachel with a glare. Then FWOOSH, she's out the door. I look at Rachel. "Do you really think it's okay to let people in who're regular?"

Rachel laughs. "How do you know Sagal's regular? And even if she is, why turn away from solidarity? What exactly happened?"

"Vandal McDaniel tried to rip off her hijab."

Rachel's jaw sets. "Did anyone try to stop him?"

"Evidently not."

"Did a teacher see what was going on?" Her brain is making calculations.

"Dearborn. But she didn't do anything. Ask Rose."

"I will." Her face is full of storm clouds.

I honestly don't like looking at Rachel right now. But she puts her anger away before it overtakes her. She smiles, though her face is still stormy.

Rachel goes back to the band room. I'm left to slip back into the crowd in the hall.

FWOOSH.

After I go to my locker to grab my cookbook for FACS—that's Family and Consumer Science, previously known as Home Ec, also known as How to Make Snacks in

School—I have to walk by Dearborn's classroom. I give her a level stare, and she smiles. Her eyes are still cold. I walk by Vandal, who's leaning on the wall outside the library, about ten feet down from Dearborn's door, talking to the dudes who love to drive around in his brand-new pickup truck and play with the SiriusXM stations. I glare at him, and he smiles like a wolf might.

"What's new, Evvie?" He looks at me in a way that says *I am the boss in any and all situations.* He looks like he stepped out of the window of Abercrombie & Fitch.

"Pulling off someone's hijab is really low, even for you."

Bigger smile. "It didn't come all the way off, and who cares if I see her hair?"

"You're an asshole, plain and simple."

"Evvie!" Dearborn heard me. "That language is inappropriate."

I flip him the swear finger, resisting the urge to turn it toward Dearborn, and head into the classroom.

I took FACS to fill up my schedule instead of having a pointless study hall, and mostly it's uninspired. But today, I beat the shit out of some eggs, and that's satisfying.

All I can see is Sagal's face. All I can feel is the disconnect between Sam's flute notes and Vandal's attack.

I HATE having emotions the size and depth of Lake Superior.

Why isn't Vandal's kind of shit a high-stakes situation? As in, his behavior will lead him down a bad road, now he's pulling off hijabs but he could become a felon, we have to stop him before he becomes a rapist—something like that?

Nah. Just a kid having fun.

I beat some more eggs.

Eleven thirty p.m. Blue texts me while I'm thinking about homework, thinking about going to bed, and thinking about a snack, while doing none of that.

PELAGIC BLUE: how was school?

> **OCTO GIRL:** the hateful teacher
> who wants me to write about foxes
> watched a student get attacked
> today and did NOTHING.

PELAGIC BLUE: this world sucks.

> **OCTO GIRL:** agreed.

Then it's just a string of weird emojis.

> **OCTO GIRL:** um . . . Blue?

Pause.

> **OCTO GIRL:** you okay?

PELAGIC BLUE: rough day on my end,
too. freaky brain.

We've never talked about this, so I tread lightly.

> **OCTO GIRL:** you, too, have an
> unruly brain? that's what I call
> mine.

PELAGIC BLUE: sometimes. if I tell you
about it, you won't want to go to Zoo
Prom with me, so don't even ask.
☹☹☹☹☹☹☹

> **OCTO GIRL:** i'm a safe person
> to tell. just know that. of course
> i'll want to go to Zoo Prom
> with you!

PELAGIC BLUE: we'll see. ☹
just wanted some human chat for a
moment. gotta go.

He'd probably fit into the Lair.

That makes me like him even more.

I text Ken.

> **<3 <3 <3:** how do you help a boy feel better?

FILM DIVA: blow jobs.

> **<3 <3 <3:** 😭😭😭 not like that. emotionally.

FILM DIVA: same answer.

> **<3 <3 <3:** you off your face?

Obviously it's a Pink Whitney night.

FILM DIVA: maybe. maybe not. you can't help people with their emotions. they just suck. did you watch my littering clip?

> **<3 <3 <3:** yes! i told you! that and composting. they're good!

FILM DIVA: oh yeah. too much relaxing juice.

Then there's a photo of a grown-up size bottle of Pink Whitney with not much in it. love you. emotions suck. go to bed.

So I do.

But I lay awake and think about Blue. And Ken. And brains.

POSSIBLE WAYS TO COMFORT A HURTING FRIEND WHO'S A BOY

1. Blow jobs—no (also no titty pics)
2. Cheerful texts—insensitive (funny selfies— also insensitive)
3. Cards in the mail (do people really do that? What's his address?)
4. Ice-cream date (though we can't go right now)
5. Monster truck show tickets (gag)
6. Bottle of Pink Whitney (blargh, don't be gross)
7. Vikes/T-wolves/Wild tickets (with what $?)
8. Videos of Popcorn

So I make a video of Popcorn—once I wake her up and get her some kitty yummies, that is. She flips out when I get out the feather toy, and then she collapses onto my lap, purring like the machine she is.

Send.

Five minutes go by.

PELAGIC BLUE: cute orb.

> **OCTO GIRL:** she's just...fluffy.

PELAGIC BLUE: bonus points for
including a cat.

> **OCTO GIRL:** any pets at your place?

PELAGIC BLUE: just T the DB.

Then there's a photo of a betta fish, who's absolutely
gorgeous.

> **OCTO GIRL:** why do you call your
> fish T the DB?

PELAGIC BLUE: his name is Terrence.
he's been keeping me company since
the end of eighth grade, and to me, he's
always looked like a drag queen, with
his fancy, fluffy-wavy fins and tail, all
those colors. T the DB = Terrence the
Drag Betta.

> **OCTO GIRL:** seems perfect for a
> fish nerd like you ☺ ☺

PELAGIC BLUE: he's fun, even though
he's just a fish. my constant companion.

> **OCTO GIRL:** is any fish just a fish?

PELAGIC BLUE: nah. they're way
smarter than we think. now go to bed.
it's late. don't waste any more time on a
loser like me.

> **OCTO GIRL:** hush it. fake news.
> good night to you and T the DB.

I look at the clock. It's 1:45 a.m.
  I put the phone down. I pick the cat up.
  We try to sleep.

This will sound weird.

  I have a galaxy of love to give to people. An entire universe. If people stayed off my case and just let me love, I'd be an unstoppable force. I'd glow so much, you could plug a lamp into me. I'd be so happy, you could charge your phone on my face.

  If people like Vandal disappeared from the planet, I could power Bluestem Lake.

  If Dearborn hopped off my wang, I would have enough energy to make a zillion presentations.

I could be phenomenal.

Kitty moves because I'm squeezing her too hard. She plops on my feet and starts to purr.

I empty my brain. I will it to be blank.

I look at the clock. Two fifteen.

Sigh.

Seven thirty a.m. I text Ken.

> **<3 <3 <3:** we should get together soon

FILM DIVA: you're the one who never comes here

So it's gonna be that kind of morning.

> **<3 <3 <3:** can you come this weekend?

FILM DIVA: gotta work. can you come here?

> **<3 <3 <3:** i'll make it work. chat soon? have a good day, bestie.

FILM DIVA: gotta find the advil. u have a good day 2. love u.

<3 <3 <3: 😗😗😗

In homeroom, I text Blue.

> **OCTO GIRL:** hope today is better

> **PELAGIC BLUE:** me too. thanks for
> the text.

> **OCTO GIRL:** any time, pal.

> **PELAGIC BLUE:** thanks for being my pal. 🙂

Am I his only pal?
Does he have no pals?

7

THURSDAY. SAM IS DOING PULL-UPS WITH THE BAR WHILE HE WAITS FOR LUNCH to be over.

"Seventeen…eighteen…nineteen…twenty." He drops down. "I need to get to two hundred pull-ups this week, and since I don't have a bar at home I have to do it here, and this week I'm gonna be really busy because we're doing so much lifting for track, and…" He's already at 175. Rachel put the bar between two of the cabinets three years ago for Sam's older brother, Sawyer, to do the very same thing.

Gus Gus is still reading *A Brief History of Time*, though he's further along. He doesn't look up while Sam talks, because Sam talks a lot—to the air and the room and anyone in earshot, same way he plays the flute. We all just respond whenever it seems appropriate, or when we're spoken to directly.

"How's your octopus, Evvie? What's her name again?" He's putting on deodorant.

"Aretha."

"Like Aretha Franklin?"

"Yup."

He nods. "My dad listened to Aretha's gospel records for a month after she died." He rummages in the snack box and pulls out a chocolate chip granola bar. "My mom told me she ate these every day when she was in college."

I hear a key, and Rose opens the door a crack to slip in. The keys go back to the start of the Lair, and when kids graduate, they pass them on to the Lair occupants who come after them. Tradition says that only juniors and seniors can have keys. Right now that's me, Gus Gus, and Rose. Sam will get his next year—I'm going to give him mine.

Rose's face tells us something excellent has just gone down. "Guess what happened to Dearborn?"

Gus Gus looks up at the ceiling. "Rachel knows." And he goes back to his book, without another word.

"Why would Rachel know what happened to Dearborn?" Rose gives Gus Gus a look.

"I heard her laughing with Carl the Custodian, and

they said Dearborn's name a couple times." Still looking at Stephen Hawking.

"When was this?"

"An hour ago." Back to his book.

Carl the Custodian is the coolest dude at school. My mom always says if you're going to get anywhere in life, you need to be friends with administrative assistants and custodians because they're literally the people who see and know everything. Carl is the perfect example of this idea. He might be...sixty? Seventy? He jumps kids' cars in the winter, or when they forget to shut off their lights. He has snowball fights with us. Faculty and staff call him Carl the Custodian, too, and he was here when my mom was.

"So what was it, Rose?" My mind got derailed with Carl.

Rose rummages in the snack box. "Someone left a message on her board. Pretty direct."

"A note?"

"On the board, in giant colorful letters. 'We saw you. Do better. Protect students. No bullying.' With drawings of flowers, stars, balloons, and hearts, like a middle school girl did it."

"I bet Dearborn was pissed."

Rose smiles. "She's not a fan of being called out. It must've happened during the pep rally."

We sent three golfers to state today instead of having homeroom. Dearborn's room was empty for maybe twenty minutes.

"Interesting." I dig for a granola bar.

"Provocative." Sam grabs another chocolate chip one.

"Curious." Gus Gus doesn't look up.

"Intriguing." Rose smiles again after she's found her CLIF Bar.

I make a mental note to come back and talk to Rachel after school.

Lunch ends, and we head out to the afternoon's frivolity. FWOOSH. Except for Gus Gus, that is, who's doing his unofficial job, anchoring our peaceful place. After I get my books, I slide by Dearborn's class to see what I can see. She has a sour look on her face and is shooing people past her door. Word's gotten around, obviously. I'm sure the board's erased by now.

I step on something—turns out to be a pencil—and when I bend down to pick it up, I see the *M* sticker at the bottom of her door. It's pretty simple—a small white sticker, no bigger than a quarter, right above the floor, on the metal doorframe. It's got a black *M* on it.

I've seen that sticker somewhere else.

It prickles the back of my mind for the rest of the day.

Rachel looks up when I appear in her doorway after the final bell rings. "Hey. How are you?" She's sitting behind her desk, working on her laptop. She looks stressed.

"Great, after I found out about Dearborn and her whiteboard. How the hell did that happen?"

She smiles in a way I've not seen before, and I thought I'd seen all of Rachel's facial expressions. "People took it pretty seriously when she didn't help Sagal."

"So that wasn't the work of a kid?"

Rachel shrugs and lowers her eyes to her laptop. "I'm not at liberty to say." The stressed look is back.

"What does that mean?"

She shrugs again but doesn't look at me. "Have a good night, okay, Evvie? Let me know how it's going with your Aretha report. As a teacher, I should encourage you to follow Dearborn's directions, but I know you. Remember, there might be consequences for not following them."

"Yup, but it'll be so good, she can't resist it."

"Okay, Evvie. Later." She keeps working.

"You all right, Rachel?"

"Just totally, completely, and utterly overwhelmed. Some days are more unruly than others." A small smile flickers on, then off her face. "I know you get it."

"I do. It will be better tomorrow."

"Possibly. Now go." She shoos me away with her hand.

As I turn to go, I notice there's a small white sticker, no bigger than a quarter, on the corner of her laptop. It's got a black *M* on it.

I drive home—no Aretha today—and think about that.

Later on, I message Rachel. She won't let us friend her on social media, but she's got a GroupMe list going for Lair kids, just like she does for her pep band and marching band kids. She told us not to bug her too much, but I'm not necessarily successful.

> **EVVIE:** So what does the white sticker with the M on it mean?

RACHEL: What sticker? 😆

> **EVVIE:** The one on your computer. The one on Dearborn's doorframe.

RACHEL: The Mutiny never reveals its secrets. 😆😆😆😼

> **EVVIE:** The Mutiny? What the flipping hell?

RACHEL: Someday I'll tell you.

EVVIE: Someday is today!

😲😲😲 Just for grown-ups? Who gets to join? Who are the members?

RACHEL: 😆😆😆😆😆😆

To answer you: yes, by invitation only, and people you know. Go to bed.

EVVIE: NOT FUNNY, RACHEL.

RACHEL: 😆😆😆

Teachers shouldn't be bigger smart-asses than their students.

8

IT'S AN ARETHA DAY, AND I SPEND MY TIME FEEDING HER, PETTING HER—THE octopus equivalent—watching her open the most complex box she's tackled yet, and helping Lucie clean some tanks. The zoo closes at six, so I'm home around six forty-five. When I walk in, my mom's got her head down on her arms, on the table. Popcorn is curling around her feet, asking to be fed in a voice that tells us she's starving, can't we see that? We are the meanest humans on the planet.

"Mom?" My heart drops into my shoes.

"I'm okay. Just...yeah. I'm fried." She waves her hand at me. "Feed Popcorn, would you, please?"

I get the kitty crunchies and give Popcorn the

appropriate amount. Her meow quickly turns into a purr. Popcorn is not stingy with her purrs, which makes her the best kind of kitty.

I sit at the table when I'm done filling up Popcorn's water dish. "What's wrong?"

"Just one of those days when I suck."

I give her arm a small shove. "That's my every day."

She looks up and gives me a glare. "No. You're supposed to believe in yourself. Like, every day. All the time. No question."

"Ha! Practice what you preach."

That makes her smile.

After my mom was diagnosed, she was sad for a good six months—mourning things she could have done differently if she'd had her brain figured out—but she was also so grateful she finally understood herself that we took a vacation to San Francisco, just for the hell of it.

"What happened, my mother?"

She puts her head back down on her arms. "Nothing big. But too much. You know those days?"

"Yeah." I pet her hand a little bit, which I know will both annoy her and make her smile. She glares at me from underneath one arm. "You can tell me." I pet just a little more before she knocks my hand away.

"I left the water running in the sink for at least twenty minutes this morning. I thought I shut it off, but it was still going when I came back. I probably killed fish by wasting that much water." She says it to the table, head still down on her arms.

"Okay, you were wasteful and unaware of it. You won't go to hell for that."

She sighs the deepest, loudest sigh ever. "I ran into old friends in the grocery store, ones who had just gotten back from this epic—EPIC—trip to France, and do you think they got to tell me about it? No. I sucked all the air into my own lungs and blathered on about bullshit. BULLSHIT." She also says this to the table. "It was so embarrassing."

"Talking too much, check. But you should be apologizing to the fish instead of those people—your talking won't kill them."

She hits me again, not taking her head from her arms. "I also lost my key to my office at school. It's a hundred dollars to replace a university key."

"Ouch." My guess is we don't have that hundred dollars. "Can I get you a key chain for the new one?"

"Already taken care of, and I was late to my thesis-committee meeting on top of it all. You know how Midwesterners feel about grown-ups who are late." She lifts, then bangs her head on the table, slowly. THUMP. THUMP. "I'm so sorry I passed this defective melon on to you."

"First of all, you know it's not defective, and second,

I'm not. Remember, we have the evolutionary advantage for creativity and a highly adaptable skill set prized by our hunting-and-gathering ancestors. Our brains just don't fit the society the Puritans created, which is why people think we're failures. Also remember, different isn't unlikable, bad, or defective. It's just different." She said these lines to me once a day when I was having my bad year.

"Yes. True. But today it's ... too huge."

"You might also remember our brains are super great at blowing things out of proportion, and extra extra super great at enormous emotions. And that the standards society sets aren't 'normal,' they're just common. Standards can and should change. Society is not a useful measuring stick. How many times have you said these sentences to me?"

"Too many to count, you teenage girl. But you get to have your feelings, no matter what they are." She still doesn't pull her head out of her arms.

"You do, too." I give her arm one more stroke before she can thump me again. "Your overwhelm will subside." I've said this to two grown-ups in the last two days.

"It never happens fast enough." Her shoulders slump even more. I can't see her face, so I don't know if she's crying. I hope not. If she is, then I have to cry, too.

I kiss the back of her head. "What is it that you say to me when I feel like this?"

She's quiet.

"Tell me, you wild grown-up with the teenage brain."

"I say, 'I know sometimes it's tough to be you, but I wouldn't want you any other way. I love you exactly as you are. Exactly. You are worthy because you are alive, not because of what you do or don't do. The way your brain works is a feature of your programming, not a bug in the software, and you'll figure out how to use it to make this world a better place.'"

"Good job!" I chuckle.

She pulls her head off the table and reaches for me. I think she's going to give me a swat, but she pulls me into a hug, and it's really tight. When she pulls away, I can see her puffy eyes.

I keep my tears in check. "Tell me something good that happened today." I get up and start looking around for what I can fix for supper. We have a roast chicken and some store-bought mashed potatoes.

She sighs. "I had my thesis proposal approved, even though I was late to the meeting."

"That's excellent." I pat-pat-pat on her arm one last time. "Life's always a mix. Remember? You say that to me, too. Gotta take the bad with the good."

"Who knew you've actually been listening?" She gets up from her chair and gets stuff out of the fridge to add to the potatoes—sour cream, butter, cream cheese. We're extra around here, and not just about our emotions.

"Blah blah blah." I pull a piece of chicken skin off the bird and give it to the very meowy Popcorn, who's sure she's never eaten in her life now that she's smelled the chicken.

"I love you, Evvie." She reaches over and kisses my cheek.

"You're the best mom ever. Never forget." I kiss her cheek in return.

"LOL."

And we make supper. Then we watch a silly movie, because it's Friday and nobody wants to do homework, nor should we have to, because it's Friday.

Some days suck righteous, righteous ass. But that's true for any human.

Saturday. I drive to Apple Valley. Ken and I get coffee and bagels and sit in a park and laugh and laugh while we shiver in the chilly sunshine. It's really nice to see her.

She tells me about looking at Chicago with Google Street View, looking at the buildings on the DePaul campus, and it almost makes me sad not to be going to school.

Almost.

When I come home to do my stupid homework, my mom is studying and is back to her mom-self, no trace of the sad woman from yesterday.

Which is good. I need her to be the mom most of the time. I can trade once in a while.

My mom never tells anyone her diagnosis, just like most Lair kids. You'd be able to find our diagnoses in our school records or mom's if you had her medical records. But just like us, she knows that if we tell people, the stereotypes start IMMEDIATELY.

People think Sam's smoking meth, because he's so hyper. People think Rose is a space case. Gus Gus is dumb. On and on. Blue told me people think he's a serial killer, because he's almost always frowning, trying to get his thoughts together.

I wish my mom had a Lair.

Rachel says labels only matter if you're soup cans, and we're all beautiful flowers, so forget those jokers, it's our job to bloom. At least once a week she says it: *Just bloom, kids. I don't care if you're a rose or a tulip or a daisy. Or a dandelion.*

As a bouquet, you probably couldn't sell a lot of that mix, but that's all right.

We're gorgeous.

9

I WAKE UP MONDAY TO A TEXT FROM KEN.

> **FILM DIVA:** we're so close, like A
> FREAKING MONTH AND WE'RE DONE.
> i can't stand this anymore!

> > **<3 <3 <3:** what happened to my
> > sunny friend Ken?

> **FILM DIVA:** she's on permanent
> vacation. 😡😡😡😡😡😡

> > **<3 <3 <3:** deep breaths. we're sitting
> > in a park, having coffee, laughing.

FILM DIVA: fuck that. i need some pink whitney!

I let it go.

T lets me out of art because they know I've got to get working on my Aretha PowerPoint. We're drawing, theoretically in preparation for our final projects. Everything I do looks like a Michaels-craft-store poster. I just keep using a lot of color, hoping it will help.

It doesn't.

I'm sitting in the Lair with my laptop, and I've made one slide. It says **HELL NO TO FOXES.** Underneath that, in parentheses, I write **HOP OFF MY WANG.**

The door cracks open and Rose slides in. She knows gossip. I can see it all over her face.

"What?"

Her grin is huge. "Rumor has it that they looked at the videotape for that hallway, when the pep rally was going on, and all they saw was Carl the Custodian going in. And he had to fix her blinds, so he had a legit excuse to be in there."

"Hmm." My mind takes off on its conspiracy train.

"There's no way it's Carl." Rose climbs into a reset pod. "Will you help me make sure I'm out of here in twenty-five minutes?"

"Set your damn alarm."

"I will, but that doesn't mean I won't ignore it." She shuts the door.

I make a mental note to talk to Rachel about Carl. Rachel can't avoid the topic forever.

I upload three photos of Aretha from my phone to my laptop and get them placed on three separate slides. I write **THIS IS ARETHA AND SHE'S A CEPHALOPOD, WHICH IS NOT A FOX.** Then I list—yay, list, something I know how to do— eight octopus facts, being mindful of Dearborn's requirements. Then I upload a video of Aretha opening her most complex box to grab a shrimp. Once I get it placed on a page, I have to watch it a couple times. Then I fall down the rabbit hole of octopus videos on YouTube, and I forget to watch my clock, but I hear Rose's alarm go off, so I wait a bit and knock on the reset-pod door. Gently. Rose falls asleep easily, but waking up is hard on her.

She emerges and rubs her eyes. Her hair needs help. "Thanks for knocking. Where's the brush?"

I point. "Where it's supposed to be." We keep breath mints, deodorant, tampons, eyeliner, whatever a person might need, in the reset pod to the right of her. The Lair is a one-stop shop.

She gives her hair a quick swipe up into a bun and is out the door, sucking on a mint to wake herself up. FWOOSH.

Aretha's PowerPoint is barely started.

I click into our course management system to see what exactly Dearborn wants us to include. Lucky for me, she's got it all listed. The one that stops me is "any other relevant information that shows why this animal is valuable."

It's valuable because it exists. Duh.

I create an empty slide for each requirement Dearborn has and give the pages the right titles. Then I stare. And stare. And stare around the room.

Next to the door, there's a printed meme that says IF YOU HAD TO GIVE UP ALL BUT THREE, WHICH ONES WOULD YOU PICK? There's a grid of nine things: pizza, tacos, hamburgers, cheese, cake, doughnuts, chocolate, ice cream, and Sour Patch Kids. Some wise human took a black marker and drew a big three through the grid so they're all connected and wrote, *There. Fixed it for you.*

And that's how galaxy brains work.

I stare some more.

Gus Gus comes in and settles himself on the couch. He pulls out a copy of *The Art of War* by Sun Tzu and becomes oblivious to the world. Rose comes back in, brushes her hair again since it's already fallen out of its bun, grabs another mint, and heads out. FWOOSH one more time.

Rachel sticks her head in from the band-room

doorway, smiles at Gus Gus, who doesn't see her, then smiles at me. I smile back. She pulls her head back out.

I close my computer, pack up my bag, and get a CLIF Bar. Tomorrow. I'll work on it then. When there's even less time. And I have to get sources for everything.

FWOOSH.

When I open the door, Vandal's walking by with his peeps. He looks past me, into the Lair, and yells as loud as he can, "Look, everyone! Here's where all the brain-damaged kids hang out! Fucking weirdos!"

Suddenly Gus Gus is at the door, cool as a cucumber. "Hey, Vandal."

"What do you want, idiot?" Vandal stops, though his companion assholes keep walking.

Gus Gus looks Vandal straight in the eye. "When I win the Nobel Prize, I'll be sure to thank you for your support. You're a motherfucker, plain and simple." And he turns away, like he's just said *No, we don't need any today, thank you.*

The look on Vandal's face is enough to take away my stress.

"Get out of here, dickface." I gesture and he goes. Not another word. Still with that look on his face. Vandal was denied his chance to inflict pain, and he's not a fan.

His boys haven't even looked back.

Gus Gus doesn't generally bust out the f-bombs, but

I do feel pretty confident he could win the Nobel Prize in twenty years. And MIT is always in the list of top-ten Nobel Prize–producing schools. I looked.

I close the door on a reading Gus Gus and smile all the way to my locker. And to my next class.

IF PEOPLE LEFT EVVIE ALONE, WHAT MIGHT EVVIE DO?

1. I might turn into a marine biologist.
   a. All I'd have to do is study Aretha and cephalopods and the ocean.
   b. I'd solve the mysteries of the deep. I'm fully capable.
   c. Blue and I could work together.
   d. I wouldn't make anyone mad.
   e. I would still do the crap work of washing dishes and chopping chum.
   f. This ^^ sublist is the general plan for the gap year.
2. I wouldn't fight with Dearborn.
   a. She'd know I'll put more effort into a presentation I'm interested in than one I'm not, even though said stupefyingly stupid presentation is worth a quarter of my grade

and my graduation hinges on this class.

    b. Did I mention that?

    c. My graduation hinges on passing Biology.

3. I would cultivate more peace in my life.

4. I WOULD SPEND MORE TIME AT THE ZOO.

    a. I could hang with Aretha, Sarah, and Lucie.

5. I could hang with Blue (I know I already said this).

6. I could invent new renewable fuel sources—possibly.

7. I could find a cure for cancer—maybe everybody says this?

8. I could help my mom be less stressed.

    a. She wouldn't be angry at herself for three days because she had to pay seventy-five dollars for missing her dentist appointment.

I'm walking by the Hole—the tiny little room off the principal's office where Garfield puts kids who have in-school suspension—on my way back to the Lair for lunch when I notice the door is cracked a bit. Someone must be out to pee. Even though I know it's not my biz, I peek inside. Nobody. I keep walking.

"Evvie!"

I turn and it's Sam, with his hand on the doorknob.

"Dude! What are you doing?"

"What *aren't* I doing?" He laughs. This isn't Sam's first in-school suspension. "Didn't Rose tell you? Guess what I did?"

"No, she didn't, and you better get back in there."

He looks over his shoulder. "I get a two-minute break every three hours. I've still got"—he checks the timer in his hand; no phones or smartwatches in the Hole— "thirty seconds. For the second time, GUESS WHAT I DID."

"You drove your car onto the football field." A kid did that a few years ago.

"Better. I mooned Dearborn." His grin is as wide as it can be. "And she lost her shit."

I laugh. "And you did that why?"

"Dopamine is a hard mistress." He looks at the ceiling, like the instructions for mooning teachers are up there. "Dearborn's such a bitch, though. Rose knocked a bunch of shit out of her locker, not on purpose, and she was picking it up when Dearborn said, 'Well, Rose, once again your clumsiness will make you late to class.' And you know how Rose is self-conscious."

I nod my head.

"I had on easy-off shorts, so I walked straight up to her, said, 'What's up, Audrey?' and turned around and mooned her. Pulled up my shorts and went to class. Rose stopped crying, at least. I didn't even make it five minutes before dear old Audrey had been in and out of Garfield's office and he was at the door of my math class."

Sam is completely unrepentant.

"Did Rose say thanks, I hope?"

He grins and nods. "She brought me cookies last night, too." He pats his pockets. "I still have a couple left."

"You are a true and noble friend."

"Hell yeah." Sam's timer starts dinging. "Or maybe I'm a dipshit. Either way, Audrey's a bitch and someday I'll really get her. For now, this is good."

"Love you, Sam."

"Bet." He grins and ambles back into the Hole.

It's easier to deal with the rest of the school day after Sam's story. That kid constantly blurs the line between brave and stupid. And I will love him forever for that skill.

Why the hell didn't Rose tell us?

Fucking Dearborn.

Damn. I hate sitting in class.

If I was a good student, I'd wait until after school to text Blue.

I'm not. And I'm not paying attention, anyway.

OCTO GIRL: hey Blue.

No answer.

OCTO GIRL: doing all right?

No answer.

OCTO GIRL: how's T the DB?

Maybe he's in class. Maybe *he's* paying attention.
I text Ken.

<3 <3 <3: we forgot to talk dresses
on Saturday! FRAK. i need help!

One of Ken's best skills is being girly. Me? My hair is basic,
enough to be swept into a messy bun or ponytail. Makeup—
possibly? It varies. Clothes are for wearing, not for showing
off. Girly tasks are boring and pointless and don't help me be
less awkward, anyway. Why waste the time? Also, nobody
wants to date me. Even if I want it to be, I don't think Zoo
Prom with Blue counts as a date. It's work-related.

Ken, on the other hand, is gorgeous. Pretty skin, big

blue eyes, long and *honey-colored* hair, according to Ken—
please do not call her blond. She's fashion conscious in
ways I could never be, and she always looks coordinated
and cool. I'm a boring Midwestern white girl, and she's a
picture-perfect one.

FILM DIVA: oh shit, we totally forgot.

<3 <3 <3: i am in desperate need
of girl assistance.

FILM DIVA: 😆😆😆

<3 <3 <3: seriously tho. when
can we shop for Zoo Prom?

FILM DIVA: deets again: what's Zoo Prom?
when is it? do you have a date? is it for all
the animals or just some of them?

<3 <3 <3: yes, for all the animals.
I'm going with my zoo friend Hugh,
also known as Blue. it's soon.

FILM DIVA: why don't i know Hugh? where is it?

<3 <3 <3: the zoo, and you can meet
him then—we can do food before or
after. It's a fundraiser thing.

FILM DIVA: deal. so you need a vaguely animal-ish dress? cheetah print? zebra print? *rubs her hands together* we'll get you looking GOOOOOOOD.

Ken taught me how to wear a miniskirt and how to use liquid eyeliner and that damn liquid lip paint that's impossible to put on but looks pretty glam when you're done. I did those things twice in our high school career—sophomore homecoming dance and junior prom, when I went with Ken. She does them every day.

An animal-print dress is a good idea.

Does Blue want me to look nice? Will he look nice?

Should I ask him if this is a date?

Should I know this already?

Can I figure out how to go to a dress-up event with a boy, which may or may not be a date, without 1) embarrassing myself, 2) embarrassing Blue, 3) breaking, harming, or screwing up anything, or 4) talking about nothing but octopuses?

Yet to be determined.

If I cared about my future—if I understood the STAKES—I'd do homework. Turns out I don't. I'm sitting on my couch, looking at pictures of male bettas. Drag Betta is facts. They're all like that, fluffy and colorful.

PELAGIC BLUE: hey Octo Girl.

I text back fast.

OCTO GIRL: doing okay?

PELAGIC BLUE: not particularly.

OCTO GIRL: anything I can do?

PELAGIC BLUE: send another cat video.

I start trying to dress Popcorn in a Halloween costume from a few years ago. It does not go well. Hopefully he'll laugh.

No answer.

I decide to pretend to do homework.

Rachel messages me.

RACHEL: Garfield wants to shut down the Lair.

EVVIE: NOT AN OPTION.

My brain goes TILT.

RACHEL: Vandal told him there are keys, and kids have them. Garfield yelled at me. I told him it happened long before he became principal.

> **EVVIE:** How does Vandal know?
> Why now?

I know exactly why.
Rachel confirms it.

> **RACHEL:** Garfield told me what Gus Gus
> said to Vandal. I gave Gus Gus a high five,
> and I put Garfield off by telling him I'd
> gather the keys at the end of the school
> year.

> > **EVVIE:** FUCK THAT MAN AND
> > THIS SCHOOL.

> **RACHEL:** We'll find a way to work it out.

> > **EVVIE:** NO WE WONT. THE WORLD
> > COULDN'T GIVE A SHIT ABOUT US.

> **RACHEL:** ☹☹☹

I kiss my mom—yes, I know I'm a senior in high school, but I can kiss my mom good night if I want to—and go to bed. I count sheep, octopus arms, Popcorn's toe beans, and sorrowful face emojis. I count Lair keys. There are three.

I can't sleep.

10

WEDNESDAY ISN'T NEAR ENOUGH TO FRIDAY FOR ME.

Dearborn's being her usual arrogant self, with her fancy PowerPoint that shows us about the immune system and all the different things we can do to keep ourselves healthy. No clicker or phone games today, so nobody's putting in effort. People are talking about who was naked in the bushes at Vandal's party last weekend, even though it was forty degrees. He's been famous for his farm parties for a few years.

Dearborn gets louder. "Let's talk about your final presentations! We need to get you organized into a schedule."

The mumbling subsides a bit. People know they need this info.

"We'll start on a Monday. Five days should be enough to

get everyone finished. Remember, all your requirements are online, and you need at least five credible sources." Her voice drones on and on.

Finally, the period ends, and I'm walking out of the room with everyone else. Dearborn gives me the eye. I just stare back. Which she hates.

I hustle my ass to art and climb under the table. T looks to see where I am and goes back to doing whatever they're doing. They know I haven't made progress on my drawing, but I'll handle it. Eventually.

My mind floats back to the Mutiny. Can I ask them to go after Dearborn again?

My phone buzzes.

> **SARAH:** you free to do a presentation for our fundraising team about Aretha? Help them understand how unique octopuses are, so they can share it with donors? The Tuesday night after Zoo Prom.

I can't make my fingers work fast enough:

> **EVVIE:** absolutely! Tell me more.

> **SARAH:** When I see you. Too much to text. Thank you. ☺☺

> **EVVIE:** ☺☺☺☺☺☺

Then the bottom falls out of my stomach. I can't speak to a room of grown-ups. No way.

I talk too much. I say nothing important. What I do say is random and weird.

But I don't text Sarah back and tell her I changed my mind. I sit on my hands.

I put my brain back on its first track and message Rachel, who may or may not be with students.

EVVIE: WHO IS THE MUTINY?

Evidently, she's at her desk.

SARAH: 😆😆😆😆😆 They've got your back. That's all you need to know.

       EVVIE: How can strangers I don't know have my back?

SARAH: 😆😆😆 You know them all.

       EVVIE: 😆😆😆 Why does the Mutiny exist if we're not supposed to know about it?

SARAH: 😆😆😆 You're not the first kid who's tangled with grown-ups—other kids have needed help with mean teachers and

arbitrary rules. The Mutiny's been where
you are.

> **EVVIE:** BLAH BLAH BLAH BLAH
> BLAH.

I come out from under the table after I send it and get
to work on my drawing. I'm printing photos of what I want
it to look like, "in the style of" kinds of drawings. Should
Aretha be a Cubist octopus or a Monet water lily octopus?

Yes, my final project is a drawing of Aretha.

T sees me working and gives me a smile. I smile back.

Little do they know I also have nine brains, only
they're not in my arms.

WHERE ARE EVVIE'S BRAINS?
1. First big galaxy brain is here with my feet, in
   the art classroom, finding images, copying and
   pasting them. Second brain is thinking about
   my project.
2. Third brain is remembering to text Ken.
3. Fourth brain is at the zoo, above Aretha in
   her tank as she feels my arms and wraps her
   strong ones around mine.
4. Fifth brain is looking for Blue in Minnetonka.
   I wonder what his class schedule is. I wonder
   if his brain is feeling better.

5. Sixth brain thinks me and Gus Gus should go to DQ after school.
6. Seventh brain is wondering about the Mutiny.
7. Eighth brain is worrying about presenting to the fundraisers. And if I'll suck.
8. Ninth brain is listening to all the different conversations in the classroom, along with the music T has on.

It's a lot.

I text Ken after supper.

> **<3 <3 <3:** you free on Tuesday night? i need you to film me.

FILM DIVA: i'm there. where?

> **<3 <3 <3:** MN Zoo. gonna do an octopus presentation.

FILM DIVA: happy to, but why do you need film of yourself?

> **<3 <3 <3:** dunno. was the first thing I thought of. want you with me cuz it's important? want to show my mom? all of the above?

FILM DIVA: i'll be there. ♥♥♥

        <3 <3 <3: you're the best, bestie.
        ♥♥♥

FILM DIVA: wait until i ask you to
model for the commercial i'm doing for
Wally McCarthy's Used Cars.

        <3 <3 <3: no way. and why? don't
        they use big advertising firms?

FILM DIVA: my flaky-ass dad works
there now, and the owner is cheap. just
your legs! walking toward a car!

        <3 <3 <3: omg. weird...okay! thank
        you! i'll send deets when i have them.

FILM DIVA: got it.

        <3 <3 <3: 😗

This will be the ultimate in phenomenal octopus presentations. The most righteously righteous octopus presentation in the history of octopuses.

That's a long time, you know. Octopuses are about 296 million years old. From the Carboniferous period. Scientists have a fossil of an octopus from that time.

#octopusfactsFTW

11

THERE'S A NEW POSTER IN THE LAIR, TAPED TO THE WINDOWSILL. THREE copies of it. One copy is the poster with no alterations: WELCOME TO THE FIRST MEETING OF THE NORMAL PEOPLE CLUB. There's a door, with a stick figure hanging out of it, smiling away. Underneath the drawing, it says *Meet at the flagpole! Second lunch! If you're normal, you don't have to hide in an old band closet!*

I check my watch. It's almost second lunch. I get close to the window and crane my head around, trying to see the flagpole. Ten people are milling around it like something good's gonna happen.

On the second copy, someone scrawled across it with a

black marker: *THIS PERSON CAN HOP THE FUCK OFF MY WANG.* On the third copy, in purple marker, it says *I'D RATHER HANG WITH Y'ALL IN A BAND CLOSET THAN MEET UP WITH BORING NORMAL PEOPLE. LOVE YOU.* on top of all the text and the drawing. Big heart around the purple printing.

Gus Gus is, of course, sitting in a squishy chair and reading. Today, it's *Cosmos* by Carl Sagan.

"Where did these posters come from?"

He doesn't look up.

"Gus Gus?" I nudge his foot.

"Evidently, they were hanging in the hallways. Sam and Rose brought them in, drew on them, and hung them up."

"Fucking Vandal."

"Exactly." He keeps reading.

When I leave the Lair after lunch—FWOOSH—I find one of Vandal's posters and rip it down. Why hasn't Carl removed them? Or Garfield, for that matter?

While I'm waiting for my garlic and onion to simmer in olive oil—it's soup season in FACS—I fold the poster into sort of an envelope, then sneak back to the Lair and grab a container of glitter that Rose left in a reset pod.

On my way to the parking lot after school, I dump the glitter envelope into Vandal's locker.

*　　*　　*

Today is an Aretha day, and I get to the zoo as soon as I can. Blue is nowhere to be found, which is strange, since Thursday is usually his day.

Lucie has created a new toy for Aretha—it's a shrimp inside a box with several sliding panels, inside a jar with a screw top lid, inside another, bigger jar with a screw top lid. Aretha flies through it in about ten minutes, then looks at us very expectantly, like, *Too easy, and I'm hungry down here.* So we get out all her old toys and fill them up. She finishes them and then hides them in the corner of her tank, so we have to drag them out with the long-handled net. You can almost see her smiling at us, thinking, *If I hide them, I won't have to do these boring toys anymore, will I?*

I know Lucie's looking for smarter, more interesting toys for her. She's just not moving fast enough for Aretha.

Sarah is nowhere to be found. I want to know more about the presentation. I do my tasks, hoping someone will talk to me about it, but nobody does.

Finally, I get up the nerve to talk to Lucie. GULP. "Did Sarah tell you she asked me to do a presentation for the fundraising staff?"

She's making sure she's gotten the afternoon checklist done, so she's not paying a lot of attention. "Yup. She thinks you'll be great."

"That's, um . . . good. What do you think?"

She looks up. "Why wouldn't I think you'd be awesome?" She smiles.

"You two have to help me, though." I give her what I hope looks like a big grin but probably looks like a cross between a frown and a scared grimace.

"Help you what?" She chuckles because she can tell I'm feeling intense about this.

"Audience. Fundraising. I don't know jack shit about any of that stuff, just about Aretha and how much I love her, and I'm worried I'll screw things up for Sarah and nobody will use Aretha as a selling point for the zoo, and don't people know she's a day octopus and her life isn't very long to begin with, so are we sure she's the best option for a fundraising campaign, plus I always end up talking too much, and what if my random facts aren't what they need?"

I stop and take a breath.

Lucie's eyes are really big, but she blinks and laughs. "I'm sure we can work it out." She holds up her phone. "Have we exchanged numbers?"

"Uh, no."

"I'll talk with Sarah, but I'm sure she wouldn't have asked if she wasn't confident in you, and I'm sure she's told the board that Aretha's life span is pretty short. Does that help?"

"Maybe." I exhale. "We don't have much time. It's the Tuesday after Zoo Prom."

That makes her laugh. "Zoo Prom: where every-thing's wild. Here's my phone number, and we can talk audience and fundraising. I don't know much, but it might help." She gives it to me, and I text her.

She replies, then tosses her phone on the messy space she has for a desk, the one that's splashed with shrimp juice and salt water. "Five to eight minutes is generally what zoo staff do for animal presentations. But I know you could talk for an hour about Aretha. I'm confident in that."

"True." All the muscles in my body relax. "I can handle five to eight minutes."

Lucie can see the tears of gratitude in my eyes. "Thanks for being willing." Her smile's pretty big. "You'll be a great representative of our aquarium staff."

"Well, thank you." I can feel my emotions calming down, just a tiny bit. "Everything you asked me to do is done."

"Aretha and I give you our gratitude, as do the nurse sharks who will eat your chopped-up fish. See you next week." She turns back to the messy desk.

When I'm in my car, I sit in silence. I'm going to talk, semiprofessionally, about Aretha. That. Is. Fucking. Cool.

Blue never showed. That's not cool—it's unsettling, and weird, besides.

I message Rachel.

EVVIE: The zoo asked me to present about Aretha! There's an actual purpose for Dearborn's presentation!

RACHEL: ♥♥♥♥♥

Once I'm home and have fed Popcorn, made supper, and talked to my mom, I start working on Aretha's presentation. Like actually working. I get three decent slides done, then realize I need to text Blue.

OCTO GIRL: Blue! you weren't feeding rays today.

No answer. I do three more slides, and they're reasonably solid, then I make some popcorn, talk to my mom again and give her some, feed Popcorn a few tiny pieces, which she eats because, duh, she's Popcorn, and go back to my computer.

I look at all my social media. Boring. I look at my slides. Boring. I watch ten octo videos on YouTube.

What am I going to do when I get a real job? No workplace is going to put up with this kind of creative process.

Still no Blue.

OCTO GIRL: you okay? please answer.

I watch two *Hamilton* clips. I listen to three more *Hamilton* songs. It's a mood. Fifteen more minutes go by.

OCTO GIRL: i'm worried about you.

The dots appear, and my heart starts racing.

PELAGIC BLUE: i'm here. just not having a good brain week.

OCTO GIRL: anything i can do to help?

PELAGIC BLUE: nope. i'll be home tomorrow. i miss T the DB.

OCTO GIRL: home???

PELAGIC BLUE: whoops. yeah. taking a rest cure, as they used to say. got my phone back for the evening and will get it back permanently tomorrow. more then, okay?

OCTO GIRL: we're still on for Zoo Prom, don't forget.

PELAGIC BLUE: about that...

OCTO GIRL: NO. you're not going to change my mind. stuff it.

PELAGIC BLUE: such language! 😌

> **OCTO GIRL:** i'm trying to find a
> cheetah-print dress, so you'll want
> to see that.

Maybe that's too much.

PELAGIC BLUE: 🙂 🙂 yes. i do want
to see that.

> **OCTO GIRL:** get some rest and
> peace.

And then I dare it and send a purple heart. It will
mean something if I send a heart, won't it? Or am I overthinking? Of course I'm overthinking.

PELAGIC BLUE: thanks. talk soon.

And a purple heart in return.
Maybe that's not big.
It feels big.
We'll see if he texts more tomorrow.
I'm sad his brain is as stressful as mine.

Lucie texts before I go to bed.

LUCIE: Fundraising works best if you tell folks unique and interesting things to make them want to support you. That's why the zoo board told the fundraisers to feature Aretha—she's pretty damn unique. Audience: fundraisers are reaching out to families with kids. That's why Sarah thought you'd be great—you're a big kid. ☺☺☺

My insides feel like they're glowing.

EVVIE: ☺☺☺ Thank you to Sarah! Thanks, for this extra info.

Then Lucie surprises me.

LUCIE: You and Aretha are our favorites.

Nobody besides my mom has ever said I'm their favorite. I screenshot that text before I send a reply:

EVVIE: I promise I'll do my very best.

I have no doubt! ♥

LUCIE: And she's gone.

It's nice to go to sleep smiling.

12

WE HAVE TO SIGN UP FOR OUR ANIMAL PRESENTATIONS TODAY IN DEARBORN'S class. I choose a middle slot on that Thursday. When I write my name down on the sign-up sheet on top of her podium, Dearborn gives me the raised eyebrow. "Sure you don't want to go first, Evvie? Show the sophomores how it's done?"

I solemnly shake my head. "They'll be fine."

She smiles in a way I imagine a snake would smile, if it could. "I'm expecting yours to be one of the best in class."

"No worries there." I turn around, go back to my chair, and stare ahead, without focusing on anything, for the rest of the period. Dearborn keeps giving me looks, but I ignore her.

I should probably make a foxes report.

Nah.

When I go to grab an apple for lunch, I'm visually accosted by the posters on the wall in the cafeteria, a million of them, in really bright colors, with the same drawing copied straight off the ones Vandal made. They're taped on the wall to make shapes that look like...flowers? I think? The posters say ALL ARE WELCOME AT BLAHS above the drawing. Underneath, they say DIFFERENCE IS BEAUTIFUL.

Below that, in small letters, they say BRING THIS POSTER TO THE COUNTER FOR FREE ICE CREAM!

Down in the corner, there's an *M*. Like the *M* on Rachel's computer.

Some students rip them off the wall and head to the counter. Some just ignore them. Some read them and walk away.

I see Vandal rip one off the wall and stomp away. Thanks for the free ice cream, dude.

I hand one to a cafeteria lady. She's got an *M* sticker on her name tag, which says *BEV*.

She gives me a sundae cup with a wooden spoon attached to the top. "Compliments of your school administration." Big smile.

"Probably not. Thanks, Bev. Thanks, Mutiny." I give her a big smile in return.

She blushes a little bit and nods.

I take my cup to the Lair, along with a bunch more posters. I hang a poster next to Vandal's, but not before I draw a big *M* on it, inside a circle.

This ice cream is made from hater tears and angel kisses. I just know it.

I don't want to shop for dresses. But I do want to see Ken.

I wait for her on our traditional parking level of the Mall of America: P3, Hawaii, west side. I know people in other states think we're lucky to have this place, but...ew.

REASONS WHY I CAN'T STAND THE MALL OF AMERICA

1. People think it's a tourist destination.
    a. A tourist destination is the Grand Canyon.
2. Nickelodeon Universe is boring.
3. People.
4. People.
5. People.
6. All those people generate a lot of energy, and it gives me a headache.

7. I never have enough money to go to Lush, the one store I love. Everything there smells dreamy awesome, but it's a million dollars for a bar of soap.
8. People.

I hear her car before I see it, because she's had a hole in her muffler for six months.

She parks and points at me as she gets out. "Ready for this?" She sincerely looks excited to be shopping for dresses on a Friday afternoon. More excited than I feel. She gives me a big hug. "I miss you, goofball. Apple Valley is boring."

I hug her back, then pull away to look at her face. Which is puffy. And broken out. "You all right?"

She won't meet my eyes. "You know I am. Let's find your ass a good-looking dress."

"Where? How? I barely qualify as a girl." I give her a big frown while I'm trying to catalog what's different about her. She didn't look this wrecked when we had coffee in the park.

Or did I just not notice?

She puts her hands on her hips and frowns in return. "I think you're a girl who could get better at it if you wanted to. But then again, that's giving in to the patriarchy, and we don't want that. We want you to be a girl on your terms. Which are?" From the look on her face, it's clear she expects me to answer.

"Well..." I have to think for a second. "I want to look nice in *my* eyes. Not anyone else's. I want to look like a girl, but not some stereotype."

"That's a good start." Ken nods but doesn't move again, nor does she take her hands off her hips. "What else?"

"I want to...look like me. A slightly more dressed-up version of me."

She grins, and she looks like my old Ken, not the puffy and stressed-out looking one that got out of her car. "Perfect." And she turns and walks toward MOA. My choices are to follow or not. Even though I hate this place, I go.

When Ken reaches for the door handle, I see how bad her hand is shaking.

"Why's your hand like that?"

She charges forward. "Just tired today." She practically racewalks for the store directory.

"You're full of shit."

She doesn't turn around or stop.

After consultation while gawking at the store list, the only thing that sounds useful is a place called Nonformally Yours. Ken wants to go a place called Va Va Voom, but that sounds like Advanced Girl 201.

Ken pulls me down the hall by the hand. "Prom season is basically over, so there should be all sorts of sales. We'll get you looking good for cheap. Though you won't look cheap. Red lipstick, though." She points to my face. "Even if you won't wear makeup, you gotta have mascara and red lipstick."

I roll my eyes at her. "I'll agree to mascara and lipstick, but not red. That's for you."

She licks her lips. "You know it, baby. College parties are lit."

I laugh, but in the back of my mind, the worry notches up. How much don't I know?

I can't do that stuff. Drinking and weed just make me anxious. I also know how many people with my brain fall into addiction when they're trying to get their thoughts to sloooooooooooow doooooooooooooown—50 percent of us, at least. That's just trading your brain stress for a more expensive and more destructive issue.

We walk at least halfway around the second level to Nonformally Yours, and all of the dresses are for frilly girls, or mothers going to their child's wedding. Plus, everything is nasty pastels.

Ken holds up a few of the less offensive choices, and I consider them for zero point three seconds.

"You could be a jellyfish in this one." She waves a chiffon-y bubble of a dress at me.

"We don't have jellyfish, and ick." I head toward the door. "Let's go see what Va Va Voom has. But we gotta detour by Lush." You can smell that store from fifty yards away.

Ken hangs up the jellyfish dress. "Pair it with some black Chucks and your look would be solid." She follows me out the door.

Outside Va Va Voom, there's a huge red high-heeled shoe, but it's a chair. Ken sits down in a sexy way, and I Snap her a photo of herself. I'd bet money it'll be her profile on Insta before the night is over.

"Am I cute?" She changes her sexy pose.

"When have you not been cute?"

She pats the chair. "There's room for you here."

I sit, but not without crossing my eyes at her. When she tells me to smile, I do. She sends me the photo.

"How many people do you think take photos of that shoe every day?" She dusts off her butt.

"It probably has its own Insta."

Ken looks. "It does!" Thousands of photos of people with the big red shoe—from Africa and Europe and everywhere.

Right inside the door is a tiger-print dress. Ken snatches it off the rack and embraces it, then holds it up to me before I get a chance to blink. "You'll look so sexy!"

"I don't want to look like a tiger."

She walks deeper into the store, searching for a salesperson. I look around.

Zebra-print T-shirts that look way too tight. Cow-print nightshirts with really deep Vs in the front. Silver-and-black snakeskin pants that look like they'd tear if you touched them. Leopard-print bras and undies—there's a difference between leopard and cheetah prints, I checked—and then Ken's back, with a dress in her hand, holding it up to me.

"This is it! Cheetah print! Sexy!"

"I don't want to look sexy." I push her hand and the dress away from my body. "I want to look like me in a cheetah-print dress. Can we go now?" My brain's on overload, and I say it in a much more forceful way than I mean to.

She backs up, looking at me. "You all right?" Her hand holding the dress is shaking. Noticeably.

I close my eyes. "I suck at trying to be like other people. Can we just do this and be done?"

I feel her touch my shoulder while I'm standing there with my eyes closed, trying to regroup my shit. "Tell me your size."

I do, and then I breathe deep, three times. That trick usually works, at least for a little while.

"Open your eyes. Here you go." She brandishes the dress at me like it's a sword and she's inviting me to duel.

"Go try it on." She points. "We'll get you out of here soon."

The salesperson nods their approval when I gesture with the hanger to the dressing room. "Number three."

The third dressing room has a big zebra-stripe 3 on the door. Once I get in there and shuck off my clothes, I take a good look at the dress. It's fitted, with cap sleeves, a V-neck, and a tightish skirt. What if I look like a dingbat secretary from the 1950s on Animal Print Friday at the office?

Then I put it on. And it's not bad.

Like, really not bad.

Ken is, of course, right outside the door when I come out, and her mouth drops open. "That. Is. Amazing." She can see on my face that I don't believe her and that I'm still maybe melting down. "Do you like it?"

"I look like I stepped out of some 1950s movie." I look in the three-way mirror, and Ken is right behind me.

She smiles. "Add in the Chucks and it's gonna be phenomenal."

"Why aren't you telling me to wear shoes like the one outside the shop?"

Ken hugs me and pushes me back toward the dressing room. "Chucks are way more your speed. Go change."

I take the dress off before I look at the price tag. It's a lot. Way more than I wanted to spend. "Dude. I can't afford this."

"I'll buy it from you when you're done. You pay for it now, and I'll pay you after Zoo Prom." Ken's still outside the door. "Chicago will be a perfect place for that dress. With red heels."

"Done." We're not quite the same size, and right now she's puffy all over, not just in the face. But the fabric is givey. She'll look awesome.

"I'm gonna go sit on the shoe." I hear her walk away.

I get my clothes back on, pay for the dress with my mom's plastic money, since I don't have any, and find Ken on the red-shoe chair with three girls, all of them draping themselves over the chair in various sexy ways. Ken's laughing with them—she's really good at making friends with strangers. I take a few pictures for them.

"Those girls were nice, and I like your dress so much! Our dress." She links her arm in mine, and I let her because I never could have done this without her. "You're going to have a blast at Zoo Prom. I'll even help you do your makeup." She squeezes me. "You're a brave girl to come to MOA. Good job."

She knows me.

We get to our cars, and Ken fixes me with a look. "Want to go to Hidden Treasures, for old times' sake?" It's a thrift store we used to visit all the time before she moved.

"You know it." We get in our cars and speed out of P3 Hawaii very loudly, thanks to her muffler hole.

I follow her inside once we get there. "Duh. Why didn't we come here first?"

"Because you should have a brand-new dress for Zoo Prom." She's already deep-digging through a rack of summer clothes near the door.

It takes me approximately two minutes to find the best accessory ever: pelagic-blue Chucks. They're one size too big, but I don't care. I march over to the register and pay for them before another person can even breathe on them. Then, with my new blue shoes in a bag, I go find Ken. She's sitting in a recliner, reading a novel.

I nudge the foot on the leg she's crossed and pull the shoes out of the bag to show her. "Kick-ass kicks."

She hops up and leaves the book on the end table. "They'll look exactly right!" She blows me a kiss. "Perfect for going on a date with a guy called Blue."

"I thought so, too."

"Let's bounce." She waves to the cashier as we walk out. "Later, Helen."

Helen smiles at us. "Come back soon. We've missed you."

"So why are your hands so shaky?" I open my car door and throw my shoes onto the passenger seat.

"Anxiety. No biggie." Ken moves to her driver's side door, and in the sunlight I can see how pale she is. She looks sick. And hungover. She can tell I'm scrutinizing her, and she looks away. "Your outfit will knock every-one out." She blows me another kiss, looking over my head.

"I'm worried about you, Ken."

"Don't be." She looks at the ground. "You don't even watch my films. Why would you worry about me?"

That hurts. "I watch them! Just not on the day you send them."

"It would take you three minutes." She looks me square in the face. "Besties do that for each other."

"Fair! Okay! I'm sorry." I really am.

She can see it. "I'm fine. Gotta run." She blows me one last kiss. "Thanks for asking me to shop with you."

I blow her one in return. "Who else would I ask?"

"Precisely. Later, gator." She gets in her car, and I get in mine.

I think about her all the way home.

I think about alcoholism and alcoholic grown-ups I know. Like my uncle. Like maybe Ken's dad. And alco-holism can run in families.

Alcoholism is high-stakes.

I resolve to be better at watching her films and better at driving to Apple Valley. Better at being a bestie.

It's bedtime when I realize Blue hasn't texted.

OCTO GIRL: home? doing okay?

I go brush my teeth, and when I get back, there are bubbles.

I hate bubbles. Nobody ever texts fast enough for me.

PELAGIC BLUE: yup and yup. trying to get my shit together. when you're out of your life for a week, there's a recovery period. but Terrence was glad to see me. bettas recognize their owners.

OCTO GIRL: super cool about T the DB, and understandable, re: recovery periods.

I'm not sure what else to say. When I was out of my life, I was still at home. Very different.

OCTO GIRL: want to hang out tomorrow? get ice cream?

Then I throw my phone across the room. The poor dude just said there's a recovery period, and here I am, trying to butt into it. Rude, Evvie.

Thank god my phone lands in my tie blanket. Impulsivity

is expensive when your phone hits the wall and then the tile floor. I found that out last year.

When I retrieve it, there are bubbles. FRAK.

PELAGIC BLUE: Ted and Wally's in Eden Prairie? say 3?

OCTO GIRL: see you then, Blue.

And I send him another purple heart.

Purple heart in return.

So maybe impulsivity isn't the worst thing in the world.

This time.

I'll wear my new pelagic-blue Chucks.

REASONS WHY I WILL SUCK AT GOING ON A DATE
1. I will forget to be cool.
    a. Edit: I was never cool.
2. I'm doing something I've never done before.
    a. Sophomore homecoming and junior prom weren't dates. They were going somewhere with Ken.
    b. How did I get to be eighteen without having an actual date?
    c. Because I'm freaking weird, that's how.

d.   But maybe so is Blue.

e.   It's not bad to be weird. I hope.

3.   I will talk about stuff Blue has no interest in.

4.   I will talk too much.

5.   I may talk too loudly.

6.   I will worry what other people think of me.

7.   My brain may freeze up and refuse to do anything.

a.   I don't think that will happen. Blue's safe.

b.   But random people in public places sketch me out.

c.   Ted and Wally's will be full of random people.

8.   What the flip am I doing?????????

a.   At least I'll get ice cream out of it.

13

I TRY ON AT LEAST FIFTEEN THINGS BEFORE I LEAVE TO MEET BLUE. THE weather's warming up, kind of, so I settle for cargo pants, a decent-ish sweatshirt, and my new Chucks. I slap on a tiny bit of mascara and tinted lip gloss, just because I'm practicing the girl thing, then I get to my car, start it up, run back inside because the tag from the sweatshirt is itching me and my underwear is too tight, change those two things, then get going to Ted and Wally's.

I hang around outside because I don't see him. It's a good ten minutes until he emerges from his car, which is parked in the far corner of the lot. He's walking toward me but looking at his shoes.

"Blue. Hey." I say it like I'm trying not to startle a fawn.

He looks up when he's right in front of me. "Hey, Evvie." His face is pale and pinch-y looking.

"Doing all right?"

A small smile. "Let's get ice cream. I haven't eaten much." He walks to the door and holds it open. "I know going through doors is hard for you." His smile gets wider. "You made the biggest noise when you hit that glass. Even the rays stopped to listen."

I pretend to gently punch his shoulder. "Your presence overwhelms me and I can't think straight, let alone open doors." I glide inside, but not before I see him blush a little bit.

He gets an iced-coffee float with mocha ice cream, and I get a root beer float. Then we perch at a table outside, next to the building. It's deserted, which is perfect for both of us, since I can see that Blue's also not a big fan of people right now.

He stirs his float, not looking at me. "This is a lot of coffee. I'll be up until three."

"Coffee just makes me sleepy."

His confusion makes him look at me.

I shrug and point to my brain. "Opposite machine."

"Oh...I like that name." He takes a little bite from

his float. "Thanks for hanging out. Good to do something normal." His eyes are back down again.

"You wanna talk about it? I have a weird brain, too, don't forget."

"Not like this." Blue sighs. "At least I hope you don't. It's so annoying."

"Maybe we should start at the beginning. You tell me what the doctors label you, and I'll tell you what my doctors label me."

He sighs, but brings his eyes up to mine. "Maybe that's smart." He tells me his label.

I tell him mine.

His face brightens. "So you know, at least a little, that this brain is hard and a big goddamn mess. And people have stereotypes about my label that aren't true."

"Intrusive thoughts must suck ass. I don't have those." I pause. "That's not true. I do, but they just tell me I'm awful. It's not new news."

He nods, still looking at me. "Mine are...stressful. They're..." He stares over my shoulder, and I can barely hear him. "They say I should...to you and them..." He gestures toward the people getting ice cream. "It takes so much energy to ignore them." Blue's shoulders slump. "I'd never, ever do anything to hurt anyone, but sometimes they're just so loud. It's so exhausting."

He bows his head again, but not before I see the tear on his cheek. I reach across the table for his hand, and he lets me take it. Now someone who's never held hands with a boy she likes is holding hands with a boy she likes who's hurting. A lot.

"Do your meds stop working sometimes?" I squeeze, gently, hopefully reassuringly. "That's the worst."

He nods, but his head stays down. "That's when I have to chill out in the crisis house. It happens maybe once a year, and I have to up my dose or try new meds. At some point I'm going to run out of ways to level up." I see another tear drip off his nose.

We sit there for a moment, him not looking at me, holding hands. His fingernails are chewed to shreds.

I gently squeeze his hand again. "Meds change all the time, so maybe a better one will come along. Do you like your doc? Trust them?"

Blue nods again. "This one's okay. The one I had before was a clown." He suddenly realizes what we're doing and pulls his hand away.

I take a card out of my wallet and slide it across the table. "This is my doc. He's a gem. I share his card with other unruly-brain people and he pays me in banana Laffy Taffy."

"Nobody should eat banana-flavored anything except actual bananas." Blue takes it and reads it without looking up. "St. Louis Park. That's not far. He takes insurance?"

I shrug. "I guess so? My mom has insurance."

Blue puts the card in his pocket, sniffles, then takes another bite of his coffee float, which is coffee soup now. Then he looks at me. His face is clearer. His shoulders aren't slumped anymore. Like his body is relieved, right along with his mind. "Why do you like him?"

"He's super funny, first of all, but he's also a random weirdo with his own label. He never judges anything I say or do, because he's probably said or done it, too."

Blue chuckles a little and has another sip of his coffee float.

"When he told me I was going to grow out of his care, I cried until he said he'd make an exception for me, but only through twenty-five. He's got a big heart, and I've still got time." I smile.

"Being a nonjudgmental educated random weirdo goes a long way in my book." Blue takes two more bites. "All of a sudden, I'm starving."

I push my root beer float toward him. "Please enjoy."

He pushes it back. "I can go home and make spaghetti."

I sip some root beer. "Did the rest cure help?"

"Some." He takes a long drink. "This new guy at the crisis house told me I should just invite my brain along for the ride, instead of trying to fight it, but instead of letting my brain drive, it can sit in the passenger seat."

He fixes me with some intense eyes. "I'd never thought of that."

I take a couple bites while I mull over his words. "My brain would bounce around, yell out the window, and maybe throw things, but it's worth a try."

He chuckles, just the tiniest bit. "Mine will sit there and scowl." He slurps up the remains of his coffee float. "He also gave me another revelation: not all thoughts are worth thinking about. Can you fathom that?"

"Um...no?"

"As in, we don't have to give time to all our thoughts. The negative ones, especially, can come and go. Thoughts will always arrive, but we can dismiss the bad and keep the good."

"Is that really possible?"

Blue shrugs. "What do I have to lose by trying it?"

I reach out and squeeze his hand one more time.

He sucks out the last dregs with his straw. Loudly. "Your brain is cool, though, because it obsesses over octopuses."

"Ha!" I say it louder than I want to. "Like anyone cares. Like it doesn't get in the way of all the shit I need to do, and the shit people say is more important than octopuses." I take the last slurp of my root beer float. "I'm sure people question your sanity, which is probably the worst stereotype. My worst one is laziness, even though

I'm not—my brain just won't turn on. It's a pain in my big white ass."

Blue just blinks. "What do you mean, it doesn't turn on?"

"Anterior cingulate cortex, baby. You just tell yours to work—'Okay, I gotta do this thing'—and you do it. Me, I've gotta be totally in love with something, or hate it and know I'm gonna get in deep shit if I don't do it. Not lazy. Just can't get my brain started. Officially, it's called an 'interest-based nervous system.'"

All of a sudden, my eyes are full of tears. Blue sees and reaches out for my hand. "You're really nice to tell me these things. And thank you for not rejecting me."

"Same, dude." Now it's my turn not to look at him. "Same all around."

Silence for a few seconds. But we're holding hands again.

"Random thought: if Terrence is a male betta, and he's a drag queen, wouldn't he have another name besides Terrence the Drag Betta?" I don't let go.

Blue chuckles. "Good point. He would. I didn't know much about drag queens in eighth grade."

"I bet he'd pick something like Fishee Stixx. With two e's and two x's."

Blue snorts. "I bet you're right."

More silence. I concentrate on shutting up.

"So. Zoo Prom. Let's rethink that." He squeezes my hand and lets it go.

"No. We're going." I'm looking at my shoes, and then I realize I'M LOOKING AT MY SHOES. "Blue!"

"What?"

"Look at my feet! My Chucks are pelagic blue!" I pull my foot up close to the table so he can see, which means I almost fall off my chair, and he laughs, and I laugh, and the people who've come to sit on the patio just stare, because two weirdos are laughing at a shoe, and... yeah. No more serious talk. We laugh, about all sorts of things.

When I get home, my mom's at the table, working on her thesis.

"Can I ask you a question about Dad?" I kind of don't want to know, but I also do.

"Sure." She doesn't look at me and keeps typing. "But make it quick."

"Dad's neurotypical, isn't he?"

"Yup." More typing.

"Was that part of your problems?"

"To him, I was defective. I didn't care enough, or try hard enough to fix myself." More typing. "Nobody should live with that kind of judgment from someone who claims to love them."

"Nope. Would you have stayed together if you were diagnosed?"

"No idea. He's a guy who can't deal with chaos, and even diagnosed, I'm probably still too chaotic for him. Loan officers are probably allergic to people like us." She sighs and stops typing. "He's a good guy, and we loved each other, but we couldn't compromise, so...yeah." She shrugs. "You can't fault people for not having the capacity to care for you in the way you need, though you also can't excuse them for ducking their responsibility to their child. Now, can I please keep working?" She looks at me over her cheaters and smiles. "I hope you had a good ice-cream date today." I told her yesterday about our meetup.

She goes back to work, and I go to my room and cuddle Popcorn, who's sleeping on my bed and not happy to be bothered.

How does Blue deal with thoughts that tell you to hurt people?

How do you run away from your own mind?

How do you tame it so you can live?

I text Blue before I go to sleep.

> **OCTO GIRL:** thanks for hanging out.
> Purple heart.

PELAGIC BLUE: no, thank you, Octo Girl. i needed those laughs, and i love your pelagic blue shoes. they'll look great with your dress.

Purple heart in return.

Guess purple hearts are our thing now.

Popcorn purrs, lying on my chest, and my heart purrs back.

14

WHY DOES THE LAIR SMELL LIKE PISS?

Do I want to know the answer to that question?

When I come in right after first period, the smell is HUGE. I go straight back out. Monday's obviously off to a grand start. When I come in again during lunch, the smell has calmed down some, and Rachel's in there with Clorox wipes, sponging off everything she can see, including all the lists.

"Are we gonna have to take the lists down?" Maybe not the most pressing question, but it's the first thing I think of. It would be awful to lose that history.

She's got her back to me, wiping things off, but she shakes her head. "I don't think so. It was pretty close to the door, so the lists might not have much on them." She keeps going.

"What the flip happened?"

The door opens again, and Gus Gus comes in, book in hand. He sniffs once. "Better." And he goes to sit in the squishy armchair where he usually reads. Today, the book is a biography of Isaac Newton—I think. He forgets we're there as soon as he opens it.

Rachel turns around. "Some jackhole left a spray bottle by the door, and the label said ESSENTIAL OIL. Rose brought it in here before school, thinking someone had left a gift, and sprayed it twice. It was deer urine." She rolls her eyes. "Maybe in a high school, it's wise not to trust a random gift? Lair people would bring their contribution inside."

I chuckle. "I bet Rose feels terrible."

"Oh, she does." Rachel hands me the container of disinfecting wipes. "She was in here cleaning earlier."

I take the container, pull out about ten wipes, and start wiping things. The floor. The trim around the door. The wall. The puffy chair and couch, where Gus Gus isn't sitting. The new sign on the back of the door that says GARFIELD CAN HOP RIGHT OFF OUR WANGS next to a drawing of a key. I'm tempted to wipe off Gus Gus. I even wipe off the window, just in case the deer piss got close enough. A middle school kid is sitting outside on the bench, throwing up into a plastic bag. Must be waiting for a ride home. Poor dude.

There's a quiet, quick knock. I open the door slightly, and then more, and Sagal comes in, immediately wrinkling her nose. "Why does it smell like deer urine in here?"

"How did you know that?" Rachel laughs.

"Our neighbors hunt. The dad of the family sprayed it for me once, then told me all about how it covers human smells, and deer think other deer are around. Disgusting. Do you need more help?" She holds out her hand, and Rachel tosses her the container of wipes. "I came in to use a reset pod, but cleaning will do." And she goes to work on the cabinets close to the door.

"So, who did it?" I'm out of wipes, and I gesture for the container. Rachel goes to where Sagal set it down and throws it to me. I take out five more and start on the wall by the window.

"It's always gonna be the same people." Rachel gets down on her hands and knees to do the floor in front of the hallway door.

"Vandal, or someone who hangs out with Vandal. That's what you're saying."

"Basically." She slowly backs herself toward the door and into the band room. "I'm going to have to stop for a while—band's coming up. You and Sagal probably can quit, too." She sniffs. "It's way less stinky than it was." She gets up from the floor, goes to the window behind the couch, and slides it open.

Gus Gus looks up at the noise, and we're both speechless. She's told us forever that the window doesn't open. Sagal has no idea a miracle is currently happening, so she keeps wiping down cupboard doors.

"I lied, okay? Because I knew Sam would start using it as a door." Rachel chuckles at our faces. "This is definitely a time for an exception, and if either of you tells Sam, I'll find a way to get you back, even if you're in college. Got it?" She points at Gus Gus, and he nods. She points at me. I nod. "It's our secret." And she walks into the band room. I can hear the band kids coming in for class after she shuts the door. I've never met a quiet band kid.

Sagal finishes the last cupboard door and looks at her phone. "I've still got ten minutes to hang in a pod." She climbs in. "If I don't come out, bang on the door, okay?" The door closes.

"You got it." I flump down in the other squishy armchair and close my eyes.

Silence for a decent stretch. I start to drift off.

"Vandal needs a swift kick in the ass." Gus Gus breaks the silence.

"Amen."

More silence. Then Sagal peeks her head out. "Are

there snacks in here? If there are, can I have one?" She climbs out.

"Right there." I point to where we keep the snack box, and Sagal finds a granola bar.

"Thanks." She shakes her head, maybe to clear the cobwebs, takes a bite, and heads back out into the bullshit that is BLAHS. FWOOSH. I don't know if she knows that she camouflaged, but she did. She pulled back her shoulders and straightened her hijab.

"Guess I'd better go, too."

"Don't let the haters get you down." Gus Gus, my man of few words, only shares the ones that are gold. I love my brain cousin.

I go. Hating every second of it.

FWOOSH.

I see Vandal in the hall, right before last period. My camouflage is still up.

He gives me an expectant look. "How ya smellin' today, Evvie?"

"Everything's roses today, Vandal. How 'bout for you?" I smile sweetly.

"Just peachy. Always peachy." He struts off.

"Thanks for the deer piss," I call out after him.

A wave of his hand. Admission? Dismissal?

Just a bunch of freakazoids in their freak-out spot.

Irredeemable, broken humans hiding away from everyone else.

After school, I drive to the zoo, even though I should be heading home. I can't imagine Sarah and Lucie will say no to me if I show up.

Neither seem surprised to see me. Maybe I'm giving off *I need my octopus* vibes. Sarah's doing paperwork, and Lucie's working on a special octopus-enrichment toy—a small clear plastic ball inside a larger ball inside the largest ball, with doors on each ball that are almost hidden, they blend in so well. There's a shrimp in each ball.

"We'll see if she likes the challenge." Lucie smiles at me. "You give it to her. She'll be glad to see you."

I lean over the tank and put my hand in. Arms start climbing up my arm about ten seconds after I do.

"Hi, octo girl." I flex my fingers, then curl them into a fist, and Aretha just flows her suckers over me. We're cuddling. "Enrichment time, my sweet."

With my other hand, because I'm not sure Aretha would let go of the one in the water, I slowly lower in the ball that Lucie gives me. Aretha's attention switches in a blink to the shrimp ball. She lets go of me, wraps the ball in six arms, and takes it to the corner of her backstage tank. We'll see what she does.

"Got your presentation ready for next week?" Lucie leans on the tank, watching what Aretha's doing, which isn't much. She's thinking.

"I think so. I've got all of Dearborn's requirements in it, plus some fun stuff, plus a bunch of facts that the fundraisers can share with families. Can I send it to you? It'll come from my BLAHS account, so you know."

Lucie laughs. "I might not get to it until the weekend. It's almost finals time for me, and I'm cramming my ass off."

"Absolutely fine."

"It kills me your high school name is BLAHS. Doesn't anybody check that stuff?" She trails her hand in the water to see if she can attract Aretha's attention. There's a splash, and one of Aretha's arms flails outside the water for just a second, then sinks back into the tank. No arms come close to Lucie, though.

"She's struggling." Lucie's watching more closely, and she pulls her hand back out of the tank. "She's getting pissed."

Aretha is changing colors, and her arms are all tucked underneath her, working on the ball. If an octopus could yell, she'd be yelling. She'd be hollering *High stakes! High stakes! That's MY shrimp! Fuck you people and your stupid tasks!*

Lucie turns away from the tank. "Help me do this

cleaning while you're here. Why ARE you here, by the way?"

"No reason. Just…a long day. Someone tried to sabotage our space."

Lucie sees I'm truly angry, and she gives me a one-armed hug. "Glad you came to see your octopus."

"Me too." I sigh. She has no idea how much it helps to be here.

"Octopuses, on the other hand, don't sabotage anyone." She gestures at the tank. "And they sure are funny."

Aretha is banging the plastic ball on the big rock in her tank. WHUMP. WHUMP. You can feel the vibrations in the tank wall.

"Let's leave her to it and see what happens." Lucie tugs me toward the sink, where there's lots of things to wash. "You can do these dishes while I take apart this pump." Her smile is gentle. "Aretha and I are always here to be your peaceful spot."

I drop my eyes. Kindness is so unexpected.

I've got my hands deep in the sink, earbuds in, scrubbing the fish poop off everything, when there's a tap on my shoulder. I jump a foot and whirl around, planning to yell at whoever it is, but it's Blue.

He grins. "Didn't mean to startle you."

"What are you doing here? It's not your volunteer day." I take my earbuds out.

"I'd say the same for you, Octo Girl." His whole being seems lighter, different from how he was on Saturday.

"Too much bullshit. Safer to be with an octopus." I dry off my hands. "You feeding the rays?"

"Already done." He gestures with the empty bucket in his hand. "You want to walk over to the foundation people and ask what we have to do on Saturday for Zoo Prom?"

"Sure. Lemme finish this." I go back to washing, and Blue goes to talk to Sarah in her office. I finish the dishes double-quick, get them stacked, say goodbye to Lucie, who's watching Aretha mess with her still-unsolved shrimp ball, and go to find him in Sarah's office.

She greets me with a hug. "You excited to speak to the fundraising staff? I'm excited for you to do it!"

"I'm going to send my presentation to Lucie so she can check it over and make sure I have everything I need."

Sarah looks at Blue. "You two coming to the Zoo Prom?" She raises her eyebrows, like she's got an answer she's expecting to hear.

"Who would miss Zoo Prom?" Blue raises a fist to me, and I bump it.

"We're on our way to the foundation office to find out our assignments." I hold out a hand to Blue for a high five, then a low five, and he slaps it both times.

Sarah laughs at us. "Better get going. I don't think they're in there much past four thirty." It's 4:25.

Blue heads out the door, and Sarah grabs my shoulder to whisper in my ear. "He's such a sweet guy."

I think I blush, and I nod. "He's my first real date. If we can count this as a date."

She looks shocked. "I thought you'd be an old pro at this, Evvie. You're so funny and smart! And adorable, besides." She squeezes my shoulder again.

I don't even know what to say.

Blue is back in the doorway. He must have realized I wasn't behind him. "They're gonna be gone if we don't get there." He doesn't look impatient—more like amused.

"Sarah was just sharing octopus facts with me. Right behind you."

The foundation people tell us we're going to be serving punch and cake slices. Doesn't sound too stressful. Provided I don't drop things.

We're walking toward the employee lot, where the volunteers park, and my phone vibrates. It's from Lucie: If you're still here, come see what Aretha did.

I show Blue. "I'm going back in. See you tomorrow, same place, same time?"

"I'm coming with you, weirdo."

I don't deserve the side-eye he gives me.

When we get there, Lucie's fishing ball parts out of Aretha's tank. "What a stinker."

"She smashed it?" I put the balls back together to check out her work, and there are very definite holes in their sides.

"She smashed one ball on the rock, ate the shrimp, and did the same thing with the next two balls. Screw the doors." Lucie's face is both annoyed and amused.

"Aretha, honey, that's thinking outside the box—or ball—isn't it, my good girl? Such a good problem-solver." I put my arm into her tank, and it's wrapped in her arms before Blue can come over and watch her do it.

He stares. "Is she slimy?"

"Not at all. The suckers suck on you, but mostly she's just really freaking strong."

It's clear from his face that Blue's hesitant about our octo cuddle puddle.

"If you can pet a wet ray, you can be touched by an octopus."

Blue lowers *his* arm into the water, to his elbow, and I see Aretha extend *her* arm and touch him gently with the tip. Blue flinches slightly, but she wraps the end of her arm around his wrist. She's got me with three and him with one, because somehow she knows he's not sure.

"Maybe she's trying to convince you she's all right." I don't know why else she'd only have his wrist, but it's also not wise to give human emotions to an animal. "Or maybe you taste funny, and she's being polite."

Blue's eyes are wide. "So damn strong. Even just around my wrist."

"'Intense' is her middle name."

We stay like this for a little bit, but then both Lucie and Sarah have to leave, so it's time to clear out for the night. I gently extract my arm, and when I do, Aretha lets go of Blue's wrist. She never made a move to hold more of his hand.

"Bye, sugar girl." I blow a kiss to the tank. "Bye, Sarah and Lucie."

"Bye, you two!" Lucie waves. Sarah blows a kiss in our direction.

On the way through the building, Blue grabs my hand and holds it.

Like an octopus hasn't just been holding it.

Like it's not covered in salt water.

Like he's been doing it forever, not just since Saturday, when we did it a tiny bit.

Like we've been a couple for years.

Are we a couple now?

I don't say anything. I just hold his hand back.

Why does holding hands seem like such a big deal?

He pushes open the glass door with his other hand so he doesn't have to let go of mine. We come to my car first.

"Where's yours?" I look around, pretending to know what I'm searching for, since I've only seen it once.

"Right there." He points a couple rows away to an old Jeep with his other hand. He still hasn't let go of mine. "I haven't had my license very long. Driving tests are too stressful."

"Same and same."

He doesn't look away from my face. "Are you going to college next year?"

"No. Gap year. Gonna work here as an aquarium assistant." I am locked into his eyes, and it's trippy.

He chuckles. "More samesies. Did Lucie tell you what she did for me?"

"No."

"Has she told you about the Maui Ocean Center?"

"Where she studied octopuses?"

"I've been there a couple times with my parents, on family trips. Lucie thought it would make good gap year work, even if I was just doing cleaning stuff. There was a service job open in February, and I applied, even though I told them I couldn't leave until after graduation. She wrote a letter to her old boss for me! Can you believe that?"

"Absolutely." Lucie is one of the kindest people I know.

"I did a FaceTime interview three weeks ago. Now I think about living on Maui." His face is dreamy but excited, and more than kind of handsome. But I don't say that.

"It would be amazing! I'd miss you, though." I squeeze his hand.

Maybe I shouldn't have said that.

He looks at me, and I see no trace of the guy who was so sad on Saturday, though I'm sure he's still in there. He looks like he knows what he wants in the world and is fully capable of getting it all. "You'd miss me?"

"Sure." I don't blush, so maybe it's a reality now for my body that I like him. "Would you miss me?"

Blue laughs, picks up my other hand, and squeezes them both. "Of course." Then he sighs. "But I want to be real here, Evvie. I'm not a dating kind of guy."

I laugh. Loudly.

Blue takes a step back, like I've punched him, even though he's still holding my hands. "I'm just being honest."

"No! I'm sorry!" I try to get myself together. "That was relief. I wouldn't call myself a dating kind of girl."

His face opens back up again. "Oh. Gotcha."

"Let's just…let's just go to Zoo Prom and see what happens. Two pals serving cake and punch, and maybe going to Perkins after. That sound all right?"

"Yeah. That works." He squeezes my hands again, then pulls me in for a hug.

And then we hug. For a while.

He smells good. He feels good.

Then he moves backward so fast, I almost fall over.

"Yeah, so, all right. Yeah." He's grinning but also running away. "I'll see you tomorrow, maybe, right back here."

I wave. "I'll come by the ray pool if I don't see you elsewhere."

"Yeah. Good. All right. See ya!" And he practically sprints to his Jeep.

I get in my car, crank up some disco, just for fun, and wonder if we'll have to dance at Zoo Prom.

Around midnight, I send my PowerPoint to Lucie. I went over it super carefully because I want her to be impressed. I wish I could make myself do that with regular homework.

My phone vibrates.

> **PELAGIC BLUE:** can't believe I'm
> saying this, but—just a guess—i'm
> probs an awkward kisser.

> > **OCTO GIRL:** 😳 we'll be awkward
> > together. you're a goofball.

> **PELAGIC BLUE:** and? so? what's new?

> > **OCTO GIRL:** you're thinking too
> > hard. that's all i'm saying.

While I brush my teeth, I text Ken.

> **<3 <3 <3:** best make-out advice?

FILM DIVA: 😆😆😆😆😆😆😆😆😆
you're not seriously asking this question.

> **< 3 <3 <3:** i'm not a sophisticate
> like you.

FILM DIVA: you'll get the hang of it
pretty quickly. 😆😆

> **<3 <3 <3:** blue says he's an
> awkward kisser

FILM DIVA: 😳😳😳 he honestly admitted that?

> **<3 <3 <3:** dude has balls.

FILM DIVA: i guess. maybe you'll get to
feel them.

> **<3 <3 <3:** maybe.

I would never be so bold.

FILM DIVA: 😃😆🤭🍆🍆🍆🍆🍆

That's the old Ken texting me.

> **<3 <3 <3:** let's hang out this
> weekend?

FILM DIVA: going to a festival with pals.
music & pink whitney!

> **<3 <3 <3:** have fun. be safe.
> love you.

FILM DIVA: will do! love u 2.

Do her parents know what's up with her? Do they
care?

Popcorn settles down on my feet, and we go to sleep. Or
at least my body does. In my first dream, giant lips are
chasing me, and when I catch them, they multiply and
turn into giant pink bottles. Soon I'm surrounded by
millions of lips and bottles, in lots of colors, but then the
lips are mostly blue. Blue's lips?

I wake up when a set of lips the size of a couch charges
at my face.

This is why I'm always tired.

15

WEDNESDAY.

Three days until Zoo Prom.

Six days until I do my Aretha fundraiser presentation.

Have you ever noticed how days are like lists, but they're organized by hours?

I'm in FACS. We're done with soup now, and we're taking notes about how to budget for a family. I would never trust me with a child.

Ken texts another octopus video. She sends at least one a day.

FILM DIVA: can you use this one?

It's an octopus escaping off a boat through a tiny little hole in a ship railing.

>   **<3 <3 <3:** got enough, thanks

FILM DIVA: got a foxes backup
presentation, just in case?

>   **<3 <3 <3:** nah.

FILM DIVA: isn't it a little shortsighted
to think she'll change her mind?

>   **<3 <3 <3:** let's find out first.

FILM DIVA: don't hate me later when i'm
right, okay?

>   **<3 <3 <3:** i could never.

FILM DIVA: check this vid i made for my
English class—why we should hate Brit lit!

>   **<3 <3 <3:** we should?

I watch the clip.

>   **<3 <3 <3:** hilarious. i love grunge
>   Jane Eyre and punk Charles
>   Dickens!

FILM DIVA: ♥♥♥♥♥♥

<3 <3 <3: ♥♥♥♥♥♥♥

Then there's a text from Lucie:

> **LUCIE:** I edited your presentation a
> little bit, so please take a look.

She's noted some facts that I didn't have quite right, and she's added a very cool video of Aretha interacting with both Sarah and Lucie, rolling a ball back and forth on the bottom of her aquarium. She also added a note at the end: **You know your shit and you show your shit. Can't wait for you to present!** ♥♥♥

I know my shit, and I show my shit.

That idea makes me feel like I swallowed a star, all glowy and bright and radiant. Lucie's comment is beaming from the center of my chest.

I pick up condoms at Walgreens on my way home from the Trader Joe's in Bloomington. I bought some two years ago when I went to homecoming. Just in case. I lost them before I had an opportunity to see a dick in the wild.

I'll scare Blue away before that happens.

But I tuck some in my glove box.

Optimism never hurt anyone.

16

ZOO PROM IS TOMORROW. ZOO PROM IS TOMORROW. I CAN'T GET MY BRAIN TO shut up. I want to shave my legs and find a purse that's not a backpack, and and and and…My hamster brain is in danger of spinning itself right off its wheel.

I come into the Lair for a little lunchtime peace, and Gus Gus is reading in the chair. At the moment, it's Bill Bryson's *A Short History of Nearly Everything*, which I would think Gus Gus would know already. Sam's stretched out on the couch with an ice pack on his right eye, his left eye closed.

"What the flip happened here?"

Sam chuckles. "More like who happened here."

Gus Gus doesn't look up. "Vandal's best buddy punched Sam."

Sam takes the ice pack away from his face. The purple and blue is pretty amazing.

"When did this happen?" I tap Sam's feet, and he lifts them up. Then I sit on the couch, and he puts his feet across my lap.

"Before third hour. I was walking to class, minding my business—"

"Which you know Sam does so well." Gus Gus doesn't look at anyone.

"I really was minding my business, just saying hi to people, and Ross Featherman came right up to me. I said, 'Hi, Ross,' and he said, 'Vandal wants you to have this,' and he punched my eye."

"Did anyone see it happen?"

"Take one guess." Sam holds up his swear finger. "Dearborn told me to go to class, and then she invited Ross to walk to the office with her, so they left, and I went to class first, but then I went to the office to see if the nurse had an ice pack. When I got there, Ross was smirking and Dearborn looked bored, so I told Dearborn she could suck my dick."

I slap his foot. "Guess you'll be spending a few more days in the Hole."

"Nobody heard but me." He grins, then winces as the grin reaches his eye.

"Was the nurse there?"

"She was at the elementary school, but Marta the Super Assistant gave me this." He holds up the ice pack, then puts it back on his eye and closes the other one. "It hurts like a motherbeeper."

My mom told me Marta was the admin assistant to the principal when my mom was in high school. Marta may be a hundred and ten. No one knows.

"Anything broken? You tell your folks?"

"Nah, and not yet. My dad will laugh. He always wants to teach me how to fight."

"Why? Dads really do this?"

"He says, and I quote, 'With a mouth like yours, Sam, you're gonna need to know how to punch.' And I can't say I disagree. But this time I didn't say a damn word."

"You need some Advil?" I bump his feet again, and he pulls them up so I can stand.

"Yes, please."

I go to the reset pod with the supply box and grab the bottle of Advil. "Gus Gus, do you have any water?"

"No, but Rachel's in her office. I heard her." He points at the door to the band room, not looking up.

Sure enough, she's got a warm bottle of water, and she comes with me into the Lair. Sam takes four Advil and swigs the entire thing.

Rachel has her arms crossed. "Vandal and his buddies are over the line. Did Marta ask what happened?"

"She did, but Ross and Dearborn shared instead. At least Ross couldn't deny he did it since I was standing there with a busted-up eye. All I wanted was the ice pack." Sam blinks and winces again. "Damn. And don't bring Garfield into this if he still wants to take people's keys."

That idea jolts back into my consciousness with a horrifying THUD.

"I'm still working on that, so gimme some time. If you don't tell him Ross's assault was unprovoked, I will." Rachel doesn't uncross her arms.

Sam stands up. "So? It's not like Vandal gives a shit if he gets in trouble. We're just bugs to squish under his shoes. Same with Garfield." He wipes the condensation from his face, careful around his eye, then hands the ice pack to Rachel and gets out his phone. "Hopefully that Advil kicks in soon." Music bursts out of his phone, and Sam swaggers to the door. Music is his camouflage. FWOOSH. He's gone, Van Halen's "Runnin' with the Devil" trailing from his pocket.

Rachel shakes her head. "That kid."

"Maybe he doesn't internalize it."

She shakes her head again. "Sure he does. He just offers bravado in return, for better or worse." She turns to go back into her office. "Vandal doesn't get to do this. And Ross doesn't get to be his literal hit man." She's legit pissed.

"Vandal won't care. Garfield and his dad are friends."

"That may be, but if nobody speaks up, that's worse than the bullying. You can't be silent in the face of assholes."

"Quote of the day." I find the paper and markers we keep for lists, and write YOU CAN'T BE SILENT IN THE FACE OF ASSHOLES in blue marker. Then I put it up next to HOP OFF MY WANG, above the window.

"Perfect." She goes back to the band room to help the kids shuffle into their places.

Gus Gus is still reading.

I sit back down on the couch. "Tomorrow I'm going on a date. Kind of a date. Have you ever been on a date?"

"I don't plan to. I don't know what kind of human to date, and I don't know who could keep up with my brain. Emotions are difficult as well."

"No lies detected."

Nobody says anything else.

Ken's been texting me all day, so we FaceTime after my mom and I have a Friday-night pizza from Pizza Palace, which is part of a gas station, because this is a town of two thousand people and we eat gas station pizza. Whatever, it's still tasty.

Ken's clapping her hands like she's five and she's just

been told she's getting a pony. "Can't wait to see your glow-up tomorrow! The Perkins on I-35, right?"

"We'll text you when we leave the zoo." I laugh. "Glad you're excited to meet Blue."

"I'm excited you're going on a damn date!" She puts her phone on her desk and does a cheerleading routine.

"Have you been drinking?"

"Of course! It's Friday! I'm getting ready to go out!" You can hear the exclamation points in her voice. She grins at me when she's retrieved her phone. "Wanna go?"

"Me and the kitty are gonna read. Do your parents know how much you party? Are they concerned about you?"

"Of course not—on both counts! They don't even look at me! Too busy with their own weird lives!" She sticks her tongue out at me and laughs. "You're so damn boring. Why not get out BOB and go to town? So you're not too revved up for your date." More laughter.

"BOB?"

"Your battery-operated boyfriend! You have one, don't you?"

"I'll never tell." I roll my eyes at her. Obviously she doesn't remember we went to Smitten Kitten together last summer.

"Booze and BOB—all I need!" And she cackles so hard, she falls off her bed.

"Thanks for the enthusiasm. Gotta go." I bail before it gets any weirder.

Then I message Rachel: did you talk to Garfield? Tell him Sam did nothing?

> RACHEL: 👏 Someone else told him.
> He's going to talk to Sam.

> > EVVIE: Nothing's gonna happen,
> > but thanks for sticking up for us.
> > You're the best. As always. 😘🖤

> RACHEL: 🖤🖤🖤

I'm in bed when Blue texts.

> > PELAGIC BLUE: what if I kiss you wrong?

> > > OCTO GIRL: look online. lots of
> > > advice there.

> > PELAGIC BLUE: you've been reading up?

> > > OCTO GIRL: guess you'll find out.

Guess this really is a date.

I'll mess it up. I'm sure of it.

But I'll hate myself if I don't go.

Aretha would go on a date, if she could, and be her weird self.

She wouldn't hide.

RULES FOR CAMOUFLAGE

1. Whenever you need to
2. Any time it seems necessary
3. Not with people you trust
4. How do you figure out who to trust?
5. Almost always in public
6. Definitely with grown-ups
7. ALWAYS at school
8. Never at the zoo

17

DO I SUCK AT THIS BECAUSE I DON'T PAY ENOUGH ATTENTION TO SOCIAL media? My mom has an ancient-looking curling iron, so I get it out.

Aretha spends no time in the bathroom. She's already beautiful.

My mom's standing in the doorway. "It's been about a million years since I curled my hair." She runs her hand through her mop. "I suppose if I made an effort to go on dates, there'd be more need to look nice."

"And you don't do that why?" I'm trying to get my curls to look right, and they look…not right. I have no idea what to try next.

She snorts. "I didn't do so well with your dad."

"But you had no idea what was up with your brain. Now you do, so it might be a lot better."

Mom smiles. "You'll go to college at some point, so I'll give it a go when I need someone to talk to. You're way more interesting than any date. And stop fussing. You look fine."

I peer into the mirror. "I wouldn't call it fine. And you need to talk to grown-ups."

"That's what grad school is for. Hop off my wang." She blows me a kiss and walks away.

My phone vibrates.

> **FILM DIVA:** you ready for this?

> **<3 <3 <3:** ready as i'll ever be,
> i guess?

I send a photo of my lips, which are a lovely mauve, done with stay-on-forever lip paint. SO DIFFICULT.

> **FILM DIVA:** perfect. dress and shoes are on?

I manage to scrunch my leg enough to get a shot of the cheetah print and my Chucks.

> **FILM DIVA:** condoms? for after Perkins?

<3 <3 <3: LOL. in my car.

FILM DIVA: 🎤 you'll have fun.
i promise. see you soon.

Once I'm finally assembled, I walk out into the living room. My mom is reading—a novel, not a textbook.

"Yes? No?" I twirl around.

She claps. "I had no idea a cheetah-print dress would be so cute with Chucks, but you are workin' it. Blue will love it."

"He better. I have to suck my gut in." Which of course I'll forget to do in no time flat.

"No, you don't. Just be you." She gives me a hug. "Be home by one, okay? I know you're eighteen, but I still get to worry about you."

"It's your job." I give her a squeeze in return. "I'm sure the prom-goers will turn into pumpkins at midnight."

Popcorn meows because she thought the word "pumpkin" was "Popcorn." My mom picks her up while Popcorn struggles to get away. *No time for snuggles: more kitty treats, please.*

"I love you, kitty. You too, Mom." And I'm out the door.

The drive feels like it takes about a year, even though

traffic is no worse than normal. The zoo closed early for the event, so the only parking lot with cars is the staff one. I find a spot, take three deep breaths, and hope for the best.

Zoo Prom is in the atrium with the aquarium that holds the Tropical Reef, because those fish are the most colorful, but the party begins before you get inside. Tables and chairs are set up outside the building since it's nice out, even though a person still needs a sweater. My mom loaned me a little black lacy one.

Inside, there are serving tables all around the perimeter of the atrium, and a little stage and a dance floor in front of the reef tank. The fish are busy checking out the party scene, swimming up to the front, then darting back if someone in front of the glass moves too quickly. Fish are curious.

I don't even have to look for Aretha. I'm sure she's in her hidey-shell. She doesn't like parties.

I see Blue standing behind a long table with a punch bowl and cups on it. A giant dolphin made of…plastic? is next to it, on a table that seems way too small. Blue is talking to two women who are holding hands. He sees me and waves, and the two women turn around.

"Sarah…and Lucie?"

How did I miss this?

Lucie's smile is radiant. "Workplace romance!" Sarah smiles just as brightly as Lucie.

"Fish nerds in love!" I clap.

"It hasn't been very long." Sarah looks at Lucie, then at me. "I can't supervise her now, but we couldn't resist any longer." Lucie leans over and kisses her.

"One of you has to leave?" My heart has a mini seizure.

Lucie laughs because she sees my face. "No, I'm just officially supervised by someone else now. We'll all still be together, with Aretha." She smooches Sarah again.

Which reminds me.

I smile, step around them, reach across the table to Blue, and pull him close with his jacket lapels for a kiss. Not too long, but not casual. It's incredible how soft his lips are. And I didn't bump his nose with mine. I was worried about that.

Is kissing a low-stakes or high-stakes move? Either/or? Both/and? None of the above?

Shut up, brain, fucking SHUT IT.

Then I let him go. "There. No more awkwardness."

Sarah and Lucie laugh, and it's their turn to clap.

Blue just stands there, eyes closed, lips slightly parted. "Hello?"

He opens his eyes as his cheeks flush bright. "Well. Not exactly what I'd planned, but not a bad thing."

Then I blush. "First kisses are always awkward. But

maybe my impulsiveness makes you feel better? No pressure now to be perfect?"

"Okay, then. Sure." He's still slightly dazed.

"I applaud your audacity, Evvie." Lucie pats me on the arm. "And that dress is fire." She and Sarah clasp hands again and wander off.

"You look amazingly amazing." Blue waves me behind the table. "Come over here and let me show you the cake."

"That dolphin is a CAKE? We have to CUT IT? I'll screw it up."

He can see how horrified I am by the prospect. "We don't have to cut the dolphin cake. They'll bring us sheet cakes that have matching frosting, and we cut those. We do have to keep people from messing with the dolphin."

"Oh. That I can do." My shoulders relax before I realize they were in my ears. "And you look...hot." He's got on a black suit with a really beautiful purple tie, and he looks confident. Sexy. But still sweet and himself. Hot.

"That's hilarious, but thanks anyway." Blue raises his pant leg, and I can see his socks. They have tropical fish on them. "Not quite as great as your cheetah print, but still zoo appropriate."

Catering people are moving around, setting things out. There's a big giraffe at one serving table, and it might be made of yellow squash? Vegetables of some kind. There's a bison at another, and it looks like it's made from coconut husks. The dolphin cake is still the best, though. So much fondant.

I did it. I kissed him. Will he want to do it more? If he does, will I screw it up? Where do I put my hands? Do I smell all right? Will I smell all right by the end of the night? Did I put breath mints in that tiny-ass purse? What if he DOESN'T want to kiss more? Is that my fault? What if he gives up on kissing because I kissed him first and he's got some hyperfreaky toxic-masculinity shit going on, where the guy has to kiss the girl first, so now he's just over it? What if next time I bump his nose?

"Zoo Prom to Octo Girl." Blue touches my elbow. "I have to explain the punch to you."

I bring my brain back to my feet. "Why the hell would someone have to explain punch?"

"Because they explained it to me and told me to pass it on. So I'm gonna. Punch here. Ladle here. Cup here. Ladle punch into cup. Done. I did my duty. Look outside." He points out the big windows, where electric candles are turning on along a path. "You can walk to the snow monkeys and back." The snow monkeys are right inside the zoo gate, and they're pretty cool.

"Nice. Has anyone said how many people they expect?"

Blue shrugs. "Maybe five hundred?"

"Five HUNDRED?"

Blue can see I don't appreciate that number. "They'll come and go. Remember, it's only from six thirty to nine. The littles have to go to bed, and maybe some oldsters. There won't be many people by the time it's over."

I squeeze his hand. "It's nice to be a fish nerd with you."

He squeezes back. "With all our animal nerd friends." He nods at Sarah and Lucie, who are checking out the bison. "And fish bosses who are dating. Who knew?"

"They must be very good at not making googly eyes at each other at work."

Blue waves. "They're staring at us right now."

Sure enough, they are, but they're still holding hands. They kiss, and then Lucie points at us like, *your turn now.*

Blue studies me. "Shall we oblige them?" He's nervous.

"Will we get in trouble for making out behind the punch table?" Those same nerves are in my stomach.

"Not make out, just..." He bends to kiss me. And it's better than the first time, because it's a little bit slower. Deliberate. This time, there are tingles. "Like that."

"Oh. Okay." It's slightly hard to breathe.

Lucie and Sarah clap, and we bow. Then Sarah shoos us like, *get back to work!* We laugh.

A woman in a very pretty black gown comes over. "You're Hugh and Evelyn?" She's maybe in her midfifties, looking very fancy and sophisticated. "Thank you for volunteering at our Zoo Prom. I'm Claudia." She smiles at us like we're valued members of the team instead of two exceedingly awkward high school seniors.

FWOOSH. Both of us camouflage. Even though it's the zoo, where we never do.

"Great to meet you, Claudia." Blue isn't awkward at all when he extends his hand to shake hers.

"It's an honor." I don't know what else to say, but I smile like I mean it when we shake. With an elegant name like Claudia, she probably came out of the womb knowing how to do this.

"I'm the chair of the foundation board. We love having teenagers with us!" She's bright and cheery, like a sunflower. "Where do you volunteer at the zoo?"

"We're both fish nerds." Then I realize she might not like that term. "We work with the aquariums."

Blue's much more smooth about it. "I care for the rays and tropical reef fish, and Evelyn helps with the octopus."

Claudia's eyes light up. "The fish are so soothing." She turns her head when she hears someone say "Claudia!" then turns back to us. "I'm just introducing myself to everyone. I hope you'll have fun. Take care!" She waves, and she's off to whoever called her name.

I sigh. "I could never be that classy or girly. Not even if I practiced."

"You. Look. Amazing." He picks up my hand and

kisses it. And it takes all I have not to melt away into the floor.

Our camouflage dissolves while we chat. He shows me the Maui Ocean Center on his phone, we arrange punch cups and cake, and people start filtering in. A band has been setting up in the corner, and they start playing quiet jazzy stuff so people can talk. There are other volunteers at the rest of the tables around the atrium. Blue and I are the youngest helpers but definitely not the youngest people in the room.

One cute little kid, who's maybe three, has on a lion costume. Another tiny human is dressed like an otter. Each of them have elegantly dressed grown-ups who seem to love walking around the room with their zoo buddy, chatting with other itty-bitty zoo buddies. We get to serve them cake and punch, and the sweet little otter spills punch down their tummy, so now they're a brown otter with a pink streak.

Blue goes to get us food, and we eat at least three plates of fruits and veggies. Then we eat three more plates of little quiche things. Then Blue eats a piece of cake and I eat two, because I love cake.

Then there's dancing. Little kids are jamming and enjoying the shit out of themselves, because that's what little kids do on the dance floor. Grown-ups are doing various versions of dances that have steps.

Then the band plays a slow one, and I recognize it as "The Wonder of You," which is an Elvis song my mom will sometimes blast when she's cleaning.

"Care to dance?" Blue has his hand out to me.

FWOOSH. It's an automatic response when someone asks me to do something difficult. And dancing might be difficult. "Who's gonna watch the cake and punch?"

He shrugs. "Everyone who wants them has them, and no other volunteers are at their tables."

He's right. Everyone's on the dance floor or talking to someone else off to the side. All the food tables are unattended.

"The song is short." He grabs my hand and tugs me onto the dance floor. Once we're there, he pulls me close. Like, close. I can smell him, and he smells very...manly. In a nice way, not in an Axe way.

Blue is maybe five inches taller than me, and I didn't notice until this very moment. I rest against his chest, and we sway in a circle.

"Is this right? Is this dancing?" I say it to his chest.

"Shhhhhh. Dancing is whatever we want it to be."

So I hush. And we make our tiny circle.

When the song is done, everyone claps, probably because it's the first slow song the band has played. They change the mood by blasting into "Crazy Little Thing Called Love." All the little kids scream and holler like it's the best song they've ever heard, and all the medium-oldsters and oldsters are doing their best to disco down. Blue's still holding my hand, so we do things that look like dancing, and I realize I'm having fun in the middle of a LOT of people.

No camouflage necessary.

At 8:55, the band plays the song you always hear on New Year's Eve, right before the year changes, and everyone claps and kisses whomever they brought, and then the lights come up. The little ones are exhausted and screamy, and their grown-ups get them out as quickly as they can. Most of the older folks are lingering, talking to one another.

"Do we have to clean up our table?" Blue and I are walking back to the cake dolphin.

"There are other volunteers on that shift. Grab your purse and I'll walk you to your car."

Claudia sees us at the table and waves. "Thank you again for spending your Saturday night with us. I'm sure you've got better places to be!"

"I wouldn't have missed it." I mean it. "It was wonderful."

Blue nods. "I agree with Evvie."

"The zoo thanks you!" She waves and turns to whoever has grabbed her elbow. It's got to be exhausting, having people want your attention like that.

Blue and I walk out to the staff parking lot, which is still pretty full, though the visitor lots are emptying out quickly. We get to my car first.

"We're supposed to meet Ken at the Perkins on I-35, by the Bloomington exit, at ten thirty. Let me text her that we're done earlier than I thought."

"Hold on a sec." He bends down and kisses me again. This time, it's a kiss like the ones you see on TV, or in the movies. The kisses I always assumed wouldn't be for me.

I still don't know what to do with my hands, so I put them on his arms. Then around his neck. Nobody's worrying about their nose. And now there are tongues involved, and oh my goodness.

When he finally pulls away, I feel like someone's whacked me upside the head with a hammer—WHAMMMMM. "Is it supposed to be that delicious, or is it just because it's you?" I'm tingling in places that only BOB's been allowed to visit.

I almost can't see Blue smile, because it's completely dark. "I don't know. I think it's just because it's you."

He liked it, too. We were pressed together, so I could feel him.

"I should still text Ken. We can be there by—" I check my watch. "Holy shit, it's already nine forty-five! How long did you kiss me?"

"A long time, I guess." He wipes his hand across his mouth.

"Not long enough." And I lean in and kiss him one

more time, for good measure, then find my phone in my itty-bitty purse to text Ken: see you at 10:30 at Perkins.

I will brain her with a bottle of ketchup if she doesn't like him.

We get there about 10:25, and I see through the window that she's already there. It looks like she brought pals, too. FWOOSH. Not good.

Once we settle next to them in the booth, it's clear they're all high as Elon Musk's rockets, with the exception of one girl, who I hope is driving.

FWOOSH times a thousand. She can't see how angry I am.

I look at Blue, but he doesn't seem to need his camouflage. He can tell these people will have no impact on his life.

Ken looks at me with half-shut eyes. "We've been here awhile. Pancakes are coming soon. Introduce us to your boy toy. The guy whose dick you grab." She reaches out for the crotch of the guy next to her, and he scoots away, though he's lucky to be able to react.

I can barely talk. "Everyone, this is Hugh. Hugh, this is Ken, and..."

The sober girl helps me out. "I'm Lila, and this is Jacob, Jared, and Josh." She points to each guy, and each of them gives a half wave.

Ken snorts. "That's my best friend, Evvie." She falls into Josh or Jacob, laughing her ass off.

Blue turns to me. "Maybe we should do this another night?"

I stand up. "We gotta go, Ken. Text me tomorrow, okay? Nice to meet you all." I nod at each one. "Lila, good luck."

"Thanks." She looks sad we're leaving her with the chemically altered people.

Blue pauses on the sidewalk as I storm through the Perkins door. "She isn't always like that, is she?"

"I have no idea. She didn't used to be." I pull my sweater tighter around me. "Goddamn fucking shit."

My insides are sagging. All of the good feelings of the night have been squished by my horrible best friend. "FUCK-ING SHIIIIIIIIIIIIT!" I holler it while I stomp toward my car. "Fucking shit, Ken. Fucking shit!" I stomp around my car and kick each tire some random amount of times. "You were supposed to be sober! Fucking SHIIIIIIIT!"

Blue's watching me expel all my emotions. "I'm going to assume she's a nice person. That works, doesn't it?"

"Sure." My ears are red and hot, and the tears are leaking, even though I don't want them to. "She is. I'm just fucking pissed." I kick a tire one last time. "FUCK!" I open my car door, throw my purse in as hard as I can, and slam the door with all I've got.

When I turn around, Blue's right there, and he touches my shoulder. "This isn't rejection, not of you, or me, for that matter. She's just...stuck in her own mind, I guess? And not being attentive to the thing you want her to attend to."

I'm breathing deep, trying to get rid of the last bits of mad. "My brain's always going to tell me it's rejection, because that's what it is, and it makes the anger worse. Because if it walks like a duck and quacks like a duck, what else is it? And yes, I know that looked like a tantrum."

"Better out than in, and I know. I read about it."

This stops me. "You did...what?"

"Read about your brain, and its extremes. And its exceptional reactions to perceived rejection. So I can understand you better." He slides his hand down my arm to my hand and squeezes it.

I don't know what to say. I feel naked, and not in a good way.

My throat tightens, but I get the words out. "I'm going to assume this will be our last date, then, if you read about my brain."

"Why would that be true?"

"Why wouldn't it be?" I push his hand away and cross my arms. Defensiveness is unhelpful, but it's a freight train right now. "I'll just hurt you. My brain jumps to the worst conclusions it can, and then I spit those conclusions out of my mouth, which is harmful to both of us. Volcanoes don't do nuance." The tears aren't stopping.

"Knowing more about your brain doesn't translate into thinking you're defective. Your brain's just intense." He takes his hands and puts them on my crossed arms, like he's touching something sweet and soft. He moves my arms apart to reach for my hands again. "You're talking to the original defective brain right here."

"Your brain's just trying to protect you. That's not defective."

"And you know that how?" He grins because he knows he's caught me.

"Because…because I read about your brain." I look at the streetlight, because maybe the answers for how to get out of this awkward situation are up there.

"Evvie." Blue pulls me to him. "We have weird brains—challenging, extra, frustrating, weird brains. We're still who we are. And I like you, Octo Girl."

"I like you, too, Blue."

"Then all is well." He hugs me tight, and I let him. My anger at Ken starts to dissolve and float away in the spring breeze.

Sunday afternoon. Blue and I are trading octopus and fish videos. I'm trying to decide if I should text Ken. But she decides for me.

FILM DIVA: did we have fun? 😆😆😆

<3 <3 <3: you did. I didn't. 😤

FILM DIVA: relax. i'll meet him again, won't i?

<3 <3 <3: but last night was special, and he's important to me, and you were high AF. so much for being my best friend.

That's extreme, but it's how I feel.

FILM DIVA: funny you should bring that up. know why i drink? get high? 😵

<3 <3 <3: please tell me. 👂

FILM DIVA: do you know how hard it is to move into a school district when you're a senior? to make friends when everyone else has been together forever? do you know how angry you can be at your parents who made you move? your parents who are flakes and weirdos, kind of like your best friend? or how hard it is when you never see that best friend? do you know how hard

it is to maintain a friendship with you,
evelyn? when you care more about an
octopus than a human being? do you
know that drinking makes me feel less
lonely? 😤😤😤😤😤😤

<3 <3 <3: 😳 why didn't you tell
me all of this?

FILM DIVA: WHY WOULD I??? you're
too busy for me.

<3 <3 <3: too busy??

FILM DIVA: i drink because i miss
you. because my parents are stupid.
because you're too busy. because you're
a shitty friend.

We haven't seen each other enough. That's true. But
we text every day. Don't we?

<3 <3 <3: i text you every day.

FILM DIVA: no, you don't. i text YOU
every day.

The shame washes over me.

<3 <3 <3: i'm just busy. we
both are.

FILM DIVA: yes, we are, but you're just
a shitty friend, so i drink.

<3 <3 <3: you being drunk and
high is my fault?

FILM DIVA: yes.

<3 <3 <3: you're responsible for
your own life, Ken. i'm not forcing
you to do anything.

FILM DIVA: but you sure as FUCK
aren't helping, are you?

I shut my phone off.

My head is a tornado.

My body feels like I've been doused with ice water.

I pet Popcorn.

Then I go find Mom.

She's sitting on the couch, reading a novel again. Weird.

"You don't have schoolwork?" I sit down next to her.

"Done for now. More next week." She goes back to
her novel, then she looks at me again. "What's wrong?
Why is your face so red?"

"Have you ever lost a friend because of your brain? From...not being a good friend?"

The "yes" answer to that question is all over her face. "Not for a long time. When I was your age, I had some struggles." She looks hard at me. "Ken? It's hard to keep in touch when someone moves."

"She's blaming me because she's turned into a party girl. She says I ignore her." I can't keep the tears out of my voice.

My mom pulls me close to her and lets me lean on her for a good cry. When I'm down to sniffles, she loans me her sleeve.

"Ew." But I use it.

"Moms are used to it." She smiles. "These brains are so time-consuming that it's easy to forget people. Ken's right about that. But it's not your fault she's drinking. That's on her."

"So what do I do?"

"You apologize and do better. That's all anyone can do. Are her parents worried?"

"Doesn't sound like it." I sniff.

"I'll call Karla and have a mom talk." That's Ken's mom. "Sometimes parents are dumb."

"I'm gonna fail being a grown-up. I don't have the skills. I can't even be a friend."

"You'll get them." She's serious but kind. "It takes a while, because there's a lot: paying bills, working, caring for kids, if you have any in your life, getting educated, trying to improve yourself, and having fun if there's extra time, along with being aware of your own trip-ups and asking for help with them, which I suck at and is extra hard if you've been criticized all your damn life. It's hard AF to be a grown-up, and a good person besides. You gotta practice. And you'll still screw up sometimes. But you'll get it."

"Don't say 'AF.' You're too old for that." I disentangle myself from her arm and go get a Kleenex. "Thanks for the insight, even though being a grown-up sounds horrible."

She nods. "The horriblest. And it's the worst kind of pain, unintentionally hurting our loved ones. I'm so sorry, honey." I see the tears in her eyes, too.

"Yeah. Thanks for being so smart."

"Ha." She goes back to reading.

I turn my phone on. Nothing from Ken, but six texts from Blue.

> **PELAGIC BLUE:** this fish swims upside down. wtf.

> **PELAGIC BLUE:** look at this dolphin playing ball with a puffer fish.

> **PELAGIC BLUE:** Octo Girl?

PELAGIC BLUE: you okay?

Photo of T the DB.

PELAGIC BLUE: Fishee Stixx says thank you for the drag name. she loves it.

PELAGIC BLUE: where did you go?

        OCTO GIRL: sad and painful interlude related to Ken.

PELAGIC BLUE: gotcha. need more videos?

        OCTO GIRL: solid for now. you're a good pal.

PELAGIC BLUE: pal? I'm still a pal? 😆 😲

Oh shit.

        OCTO GIRL: hmmm. do we have to label it?

PELAGIC BLUE: 🙂 good point. see you later, pal.

That feels just right.
We trade a few purple hearts.

I write some things down, cross things out, try again.
Think. Write again.

> REASONS WHY KEN IS WRONG
> ABOUT ME BEING A SHITTY FRIEND
> 1. She's the one who's drunk all the time
>   a. Drinking doesn't make you think clearly
>   b. Nor does weed
> 2. She's the one who works all the time
> 3. She's the one who won't drive over here, or to the zoo, even
> 4. She's the one who doesn't care
> 5. But I don't go over there, either
> 6. I probably don't text her as much as I think I do
> 7. Our lives are really different right now
> 8. Aren't they?
>   a. This isn't all my fault, is it?
>   b. Or do I really suck as much as she says I do?
>   c. Can we still be besties?

Is that even possible when you live in two different towns?

Then I text Ken.

> **<3 <3 <3:** i'm truly sorry for not
> paying more attention to you. life

here is...complex. i'm sorry for
not thinking about your feelings as
much as mine.

I watch the dolphin video, then I read about the behavior. Researchers say the dolphins are getting high from the puffer fish toxins and that's why they toss the pufferfish around—to get the fish mad so they'll release the toxins. Obviously acting like fraternity bros isn't limited to the human species.

I text again.

<3 <3 <3: let's talk about when to
get together, so i can help with the
loneliness. the other stuff is yours,
though. you choose to drink and smoke.
if you need help stopping, i'm here.

Then it's time to make supper and feed Popcorn. I deliberately leave my phone on the bed so I won't check it every ten seconds.

Still no answer when I get back an hour later.

<3 <3 <3: i love you and i'm
sorry. please answer.

Crickets.

I wake up at three and check my phone.
Nothing.

When you meet someone, how can you know if they'll be a Gus Gus or a Vandal?
What if you guess wrong?
What if they're like Ken—someone you trust, but someone who hurts you? And you hurt them, too?
Can Ken and I trust each other now?
Fucking hell.
Humans are righteously self-centered. Mrs. Buddha told us it's our default setting. Critical thinking gets us past those ideas, according to her, but how does a person remember to do that when things are intense?
I will hang in the Lair, trust the trustworthy people, hope they trust me back, and pet Popcorn.
But I can't live in the Lair for the rest of my life.
It's toxic to assume everyone's untrustworthy. But understandable, and also safer.
How do I become trustworthy?
I didn't mean to be untrustworthy.

Unintentional harm is the fucking worst.

*　　*　　*

WHY TRUST IS HARD

1. People don't think like each other.
    a. Someone might think something is SUPER IMPORTANT, and you might totally miss it.
    b. The opposite is also true—might be giant to you, tiny to them.
2. Some people's emotions might be WAY HUGER or way smaller than other people's.
    a. Mismatch = suckage.
3. Hypersensitivity KICKS ROCKS.
    a. Not a thing for everyone.
    b. Horribly stressful if it's your thing.
    c. It's a biological thing, but nobody believes you.
    d. Smaller amygdalae = not so much real estate to process emotions.
4. People hurt you very unintentionally. See 1, 2, and 3.
5. You also hurt people very unintentionally. See 1, 2, and 3.
6. All human interaction isn't either a) doomed, or b) a crisis, even if your brain says it's both.
    a. Some people are kind and generous.

    b. Maybe the majority of people.

    c. A few people are truly assholes.

    d. Discernment and boundaries are always your friend.

7. What else is there to say? Trust is hard.

8. Maybe that's true even when you don't have an unruly brain.

    a. I have no way to know.

    b. I wish there was a trade-in program.

A LIST OF PEOPLE I TRUST

1. Mom + Popcorn (technically two living beings, I know)

2. Ken, even now

3. Rachel

4. Gus Gus

5. Sam and Rose (again, technically two people, but lists of eight)

6. Sarah

7. Lucie

8. Blue—hopefully

Do other people have longer lists?

Does trusting get easier as you get older?

What's the point of trusting a world that thinks Blue and I are lazy, crazy, and stupid?

But the world isn't people. Maybe people are better than that.

Fucking hell.

18

I'M TINKERING WITH MY ARETHA PRESENTATION IN THE LAIR, MAKING SURE IT'S tight. I left in all of Lucie's encouraging notes—**You'll be brilliant! and I love this video of Aretha!**—so now I need to take them out. I've double- and triple-checked all of Dearborn's requirements, plus I've added some information that kids will love and can use to convince their parents it's worth it to invest in the zoo. If I talk slowly, it ends up around seven minutes and twenty-five seconds, so it's under the eight-minute time limit for both Dearborn and the zoo.

I'm scared I missed something somewhere.

Maybe I should talk for a living. Study communication. Become a fundraiser, maybe.

Maybe Godzilla will come stomp on the Twin Cities.

I keep picturing Blue at Ted and Wally's, telling me I don't have to give my negative thoughts any time. My mantra today is *I'm as unique and different as Aretha, and I like it that way.*

My new technique: I mentally open the top of my head and let the negative thoughts pour into the air. Today I imagine them drifting out the window of the Lair.

Biology presentations started today—six different sophomores, six presentations on water buffalo, leopards, crows, squirrels, domestic house cats, and pigs. All of the students were totally nervous. Dearborn enthusiastically clapped for each one and praised them all. I'd bet any amount of cash she won't do that for me.

Nobody had videos of animals they know in real life opening enrichment boxes.

Gus Gus is still reading *A Short History of Nearly Everything,* because it's five hundred–plus pages, and while Gus Gus reads a LOT, he doesn't read all that fast. He's occupying his favorite squishy chair. I'm on the couch.

"What are you avoiding today, Evvie?" He doesn't look up.

"Art. T knows I have my presentation tomorrow at the zoo. And they think I'm almost done with my drawing, which isn't true, but will be once this is behind me."

"Understandable." He goes back to reading.

Rose comes in. "Anyone in the pods?" She looks panicky.

"Nope."

She shuts herself inside one.

Sam comes in. "Anyone in the pods?" His eye's still plenty black, thanks to Ross's punch.

"Rose is in that one." I point.

"I need a nap." He shuts himself in another.

Ross and Vandal are spending today in the Hole— they had to expand the Hole temporarily so both of them could be in separate rooms. Evidently, Vandal is in a supply closet, staring at mops and buckets and cases of Comet. I heard his dad was pissed Garfield called him on a Saturday, and I heard Vandal broke a broom in half first thing this morning. I'm sure he can afford a new broom for Carl.

I'm also sure that Carl had a really good laugh.

There's an almost-too-soft-to-hear-it knock on the door. I put my computer down to open it, and it's Sagal with a girl I don't know. Their hijabs and dresses are bright with different colors and prints. They look like spring flowers.

"Can we come in?" Sagal is whispering.

"Of course." I move aside.

"Are the pods taken?"

I point at the two that Rose and Sam are in. "Those two are."

"Thank you." She shows the girl to another one, and the girl starts to sob. Sagal gets her comfortable in the pod and then sits on the floor outside it and holds her hand, whispering in Somali, with a little English here and there. I hear a giggle, then a sob, but Sagal smiles and talks, smiles and talks, all the while holding her hand.

Gus Gus looks up to register this information.

"Getting busy in here." I settle myself back onto the couch with my computer.

"We're the cool place to be." He goes back to his book. "Did you do a foxes presentation? Just in case Dearborn doesn't accept your Aretha one?"

"Not yet." Of course the real answer is *Not at all*, but I'm not going to tell Gus Gus that.

I know this sounds delusional, but here's what I'm thinking: Ken will forgive me, then film me and put it up on her YouTube channel, and I'll send the link to Dearborn. She'll be so bowled over by my actual professional presentation opportunity, by how excellent Aretha is, and by how awesome my information is that on Thursday she'll say, *Evvie, can you show the students your octopus presentation? It was so good you don't have to worry about the foxes presentation.* And I'll say, *Sure, Mrs. Dearborn.* And I'll play Ken's recording from YouTube, and they'll all love it, and Mrs. Dearborn will finally think I'm smart and worthy. Or I'll just do the presentation again, and I'll be just as brilliant the second time.

Right?

RIGHT?

"Don't believe the hype, Evvie." It's like Gus Gus read my mind.

"I hear you." He's right. I'm very good at making up stories.

Especially ones I want to believe.

I pull up the foxes set of slides, and I add a couple things. It would be one atrocious presentation if I had to give it Thursday.

I vow to work on it tonight.

I vow it.

Ken texts me close to midnight, when of course I'm not working.

> **FILM DIVA:** i was a bit trashed when i
> sent you those texts yesterday. thanks
> for the love.

> **<3 <3 <3:** i want you to be okay.
> i'm sorry.

> **FILM DIVA:** i humbly apologize.

<3 <3 <3: same same. do you get that wrecked a lot?

FILM DIVA: not a lot. some.

<3 <3 <3: i don't want you to hurt yourself. 😟😟

FILM DIVA: 👍👍 i know my limits.

Ha. She just hasn't gotten caught yet.

<3 <3 <3: do you know the J guys well enough to trust them? what if they hurt you?

FILM DIVA: they wouldn't do that. 😠

<3 <3 <3: and i wanted you to meet Blue.

FILM DIVA: i'm sure i will.

<3 <3 <3: are you still coming to film me tomorrow at the zoo?

FILM DIVA: what time?

<3 <3 <3: be there by 7? presentation is at 7:30. you can meet Blue then.

FILM DIVA: see you soon. 👍😊🖤 pls
don't be mad at me.

> **<3 <3 <3:** not mad. just
> disappointed. 🙁🤪

FILM DIVA: see you tomorrow. 🖤🖤🖤

> **<3 <3 <3:** see you tomorrow.
> thank you again. tomorrow let's
> make plans to hang out. i really
> miss you. 🖤🖤🖤

I think about foxes. I read a few facts.

I read addiction statistics for high school students.

I decide not to think about that anymore.

I cuddle Popcorn.

Blue texts when I'm almost asleep.

> **PELAGIC BLUE:** did you and Ken make up?

> **OCTO GIRL:** she'll be there
> tomorrow and you can meet her.

> **PELAGIC BLUE:** she'll be sober?

> **OCTO GIRL:** that's the theory.

PELAGIC BLUE: you're gonna knock it
out of the park tomorrow.

I send a purple heart because I don't really know what
to say.

PELAGIC BLUE: think a couple good
thoughts and give yourself some damn
credit, how about?

Then there's a string of purple hearts, with a couple
red ones.

Do dudes honestly use this many hearts in their convos?

OCTO GIRL: thinking good
thoughts only works so much.

PELAGIC BLUE: i spend my days
diverting myself from believing i'm going
to hurt people. trust me that some
peace is better than no peace. ☹

*A LIST OF THINGS I LOVE ABOUT
BLUE*

Do I know enough things to get to eight?
If I write them down, will I jinx it?

Is it okay to say "love" about a guy that you've had one official date with, even though you've known him for a year?

Will there be any time in my goddamn life when I won't overthink things?

A LIST OF THINGS I LOVE ABOUT BLUE

1. *He took time to read about my brain.*
   a. *The only other person who's done this is my mom.*

Doesn't count: it's her brain, too, and she's my mom.

   b. *I feel exposed.*
   c. *I also feel seen, which is precious.*
2. *He smells good.*
3. *He's a good kisser, at least as far as I know.*
   a. *If he's objectively terrible, nobody needs to tell me.*
4. *He's funny.*
5. *He's honest.*
   a. *Is it rare that dudes are honest, or is that just what pop culture tells us?*
   b. *Is it only toxic-masculine dudes who lie and deny their feelings?*

No dudes like that for this octopus, thanks so much.

6. *He knows himself.*
   a. *His honesty helps me be honest.*
   b. *And gives me courage.*
7. *He knows his capacity, which is HUGE.*
   a. *Especially when capacity gets limited.*
8. *He's so cute.*
   a. *Cute eyes.*
   b. *Cute hair.*
   c. *Cute lips.*
   d. *Cute face.*
   e. *Cute clothes.*
   f. *Cute body.*
   g. *Cute butt.*
   h. *Cute.*
9. *He's brilliant.*
10. *I don't seem to have any competition.*
    a. *If girls knew how awesome he was, they'd be all over him.*
    b. *Other people are ignorant.*
    c. *Lucky for me.*
11. *I will write five more reasons, to make this list comply with my Rule of Eights.*
12. *Cute.*
13. *Sweet.*

14.   *Sexy.*

15.   *He knows about mysterious things like the pelagic ocean.*

16.   *He's got his eye on the future.*

    a.   *Maybe he can teach me how to do that, too.*

19

I OBSESS ONE MORE TIME ABOUT EVERY SINGLE SLIDE.

I find my Minnesota Zoo polo—the one I never wear—in the bottom of my closet, then locate a pair of pants that aren't too wrinkled.

I almost memorize the intro on the drive over.

When I walk into the conference/meeting room, which is amazingly large, my presentation is on Sarah's computer, pulled up and ready.

Blue is here, watching from the back. Lucie's standing close to him, and they both wave at me. I nod, too nervous to talk to them. The fundraisers are milling around, grabbing beverages and cookies, and seating themselves around the giant table.

No Ken.

I text her: **<3 <3 <3:** WHERE THE FLIP ARE YOU? I gave her directions to the room, but maybe she's lost.

Nothing. I put my phone on a window ledge. I don't even want to think about it.

I walk to the back, to Blue. He hands me a cup of water. "Feeling okay?"

I gulp it and wipe my lips with my hand. "Not particularly. You think this is high- or low-stakes?"

He's confused. "Stakes? Can't it just be a presentation?"

"Sure, but does it matter, ultimately? Does it count for something?"

He just looks at me. "Sure it does. You're doing it, so it's important. Will it bring in a million dollars? I don't know."

Sarah comes in the side door, strides up front, and turns to look at the fundraisers. "Good evening, colleagues. Please take your seats so Evvie can share one of our zoo residents with you. I think your prospective-donor families will like hearing about Aretha." She nods at me, and I walk up to stand by her. I force my legs to move normally.

Everyone has a cookie and a beverage by now, so they all sit down. Then they turn to me, some smiling, some with neutral faces. Fifteen pairs of eyes on me, not including Blue and Lucie.

Ken isn't here. Nobody will record this. I have nothing to give to Dearborn.

The fear jets up my legs and into my torso, so I mentally open the top of my head and let it pour out. I smile at them, pretending I'm not scared to death.

Sarah starts talking about all our different aquariums—our Atlantic Reef; our Tropical Reef, where Aretha hangs out when she wants to; our seahorse one; our shark one; our leopard and sand tiger one; and our one with rays. Her slides flash up, and the fundraisers ooh and aah at the right times. Nobody seems to care about the seahorses, but I love them. They're androgynous and random and floaty—and they always look anxious, because their eyes are so big.

Sarah's winding down. "Now you have a good idea about who lives in our aquariums, so it's time to spotlight one of our favorite animals: Aretha, the Pacific day octopus. Our zoo volunteer Evelyn is going to tell you about her, because she and Aretha have a special bond." Enthusiastic claps—there must be budding fish nerds out there. "Evelyn goes to Bluestem Lake Area High School, and she comes to see us about three times a week. She's been volunteering here for almost two and a half years."

When Sarah says how long I've been there, I'm yanked back to my first volunteering day. It was in January of my sophomore year, when I was trying to force myself to go to the project-based school and failing miserably. When my mom heard about the zoo volunteer program, she didn't even give me a choice. She just dropped me off for orientation. It was freaking cold, minus ten or something like that, but I didn't want to go inside, so I stood in the parking lot. She stayed with me and talked to me from the car window so it would look like we were two people chatting, not a scared-out-of-her-mind teenager and her sad, panicky mom. She said, "Get outside your head. Go visit some fish." When I finally walked into the building, there was Sarah. And Bernard, even though he didn't like us. The world got a little more positive. Eventually, Blue came. And Lucie. Then Aretha. And now the world is so much sunnier.

Sarah grins at me while I try not to look pissed at Ken's absence or panicked at all the people looking at me. "Evvie, tell us about Aretha."

I click the remote. My first slide appears.

I don't camouflage. This is me.

"Aretha will be a great ambassador for your fundraising team. Want to know more about her?"

Cheering and clapping from all the formal, serious grown-ups, who are starting to act like very big field trip kids.

"Excellent!" And I GO. OFF.

I hit all of Dearborn's information—all the body systems, all the ecosystem stuff, and why this animal matters—plus, there's extra about Aretha's enrichment. Then I emphasize some facts that families will love: three hearts, nine brains, camouflage, uniquely brilliant creature, just like their own kids, on and on. I show the final video—I sped one up so it's a time lapse of her getting into her most difficult toy—and the fundraisers cheer when she finally gets the shrimp.

"Anybody have any questions?" Three arms shoot up.

A woman who might be in her midsixties grins at me when I nod at her. "Do you think Aretha likes you back?"

"I don't know. I think she finds me interesting, so that's enough for me." The woman looks at Sarah with raised eyebrows, and Sarah nods. "We can't give human emotions to animals, but we can judge her interest in things."

A man with a very elegant suit jacket and slicked-back white hair goes next. "Do you want to become a zookeeper?"

Oh shit. Hmm. "Maybe? I'm not sure what I'm going to do. First, I need to graduate from high school, then I'll spend at least a year here as an aquarium assistant." I grin at Sarah and Lucie, and they grin back.

"I think you'd be great at it." He gives me a very genuine smile.

Sarah points at the last woman, who might be Sarah's age. "One more question, so you can get on with the rest of your meeting."

The woman is clearly excited. "Thank you for all this information—it will be so useful to us. People won't be able to resist Aretha. Are you ever frightened of her?" Her voice gets quiet. "She seems really scary to me."

"Not now, but it took me a while to get comfortable. I learned about her, and I practiced being in her company before I ever let her hold my hand. And I always make sure to respect Aretha's power. When you have respect and information, fear usually goes away."

The woman nods.

"Thank you for learning more about my favorite girl Aretha." I give a slight bow.

"Let's thank Evvie for her excellent presentation!" Sarah's clapping, so the fundraisers clap, too. "Thanks for letting us join you." Sarah takes my elbow, and we both walk to the back, where Sarah shuts down her computer. Then Sarah, Lucie, Blue, and I leave the room. The fundraisers are all chatting and talking octopus facts. A couple people wave at us as we exit. An older man says, "Such a good speaker! Thank you!" I laugh and shut the door.

Blue catches me when I fling myself at him. "You were AMAZING, Evvie. Flat-out amazing."

"You think so?" I say it to his chest. A wave of anger at Ken rises in me, and I push it down. Not now.

He pulls back from me and shows me his phone. "I got it, and I'll put it on my YouTube channel."

"Holy shit. Thank you. You have a YouTube channel?"

"It's mostly videos of me from middle school, talking about Dungeons and Dragons campaigns, sometimes about swords. An occasional one for other people with this brain. I've met people from all over the world in the comments section."

I realize I don't have my phone, so I hold up my finger to pause him and go back into the conference room, apologizing left and right for interrupting as I grab it from the window ledge.

Nothing from Ken.

Back to Blue. "That's really brave of you, to put all that on YouTube. And she didn't text."

His face turns slightly red. "Just living my life. And maybe she has a good reason."

"Which is awesome. And I'm sure her excuse's name is Pink Whitney." My anger is threatening to choke me.

Blue puts his arm around me. "Maybe you're right, but right now, we have people to celebrate with." He takes my hand and pulls me to find Sarah and Lucie. They're backstage in the Tropical Reef.

Aretha's bugging the crabs, which is another way she

amuses herself—and Sarah lets her. Octopuses love crab, so once a week, Sarah puts a few live crabs in the aquarium for her to have fun with. She plays hide-and-seek with them until she gets bored and eats them.

"We are so freaking proud of you!" Lucie grabs me for a huge hug. "You were on fire—I could see the smoke coming off you." She hands glasses of sparkly juice to me, Sarah, and Blue, and we all stand together, glasses raised. "To Evvie, and to Aretha, and to horrible teachers everywhere like Dearborn. May they all realize they suck. May they all get out of teaching once they understand they're actively harming students."

"Amen!" I raise my glass even higher. Then we all clink.

I hear a wet sound, and when I turn around, there's an octopus arm feeling its way over the glass wall of Aretha's aquarium like she's wondering where her drink is.

"Look who's decided to join the party." I hand my glass to Blue and go to her. "Hello, sea goddess. You and I kicked ass tonight." I put my hand in her tank, and she gets it with three arms, feeling and tasting me.

"Ain't nobody more amazing than you, sweet girl." Lucie comes over and plunges a hand into the tank, too. Aretha grabs her with two more arms.

"I want in on this party." Sarah's next to Lucie. She slides her arm into Aretha's tank, and it's instantly covered in two arms.

"She's got one left, Blue, and it's for you." I cock my head toward the tank and wiggle my eyebrows at him. "You can do it."

He doesn't look convinced, but he moves next to me, puts one hand on my waist and the other in the tank. Aretha takes her last arm and does the same thing she did before: circles his wrist, very delicately, with its tip.

We're a four-way octo love machine, and my heart can't take it. The tears slide down my face. Sarah and Lucie are laughing and chatting, but I feel Blue's hand tighten on my waist.

"What?" Blue whispers it in my ear.

"Overwhelmed. Mad. Happy. Excited. Scared. Too much." I whisper it back.

"I got you." He leans his head on mine. "Aretha's got you, too."

I let the tears happen, and he doesn't move.

Do you hear me? He doesn't move.

20

I WAKE UP TO THREE TEXTS FROM KEN: *I'M SO SORRY.* THEN: *I KNOW I* screwed up. And: i don't blame you if you never talk to me again.

I text back one word: excellent. I'm still fucking pissed.

Blue texts me the link to his YouTube channel and I drop it in an email to Dearborn, trying not to agonize over every word, partly because I don't have time, and partly because Ken is fogging up my mind.

I stop by the Lair before homeroom to get some lavender to put on my wrists, after which I eat a granola bar and breathe as deeply as I can.

Still pissed.

In homeroom I doodle, drawing Aretha and her tank,

and listen to kids around me. Two junior girls are talking about the new weed store that's being built in Chaska, and how they can't wait to go when they're twenty-one. Two junior guys are talking about the turkey hunting they did last weekend.

Nobody's talking about their best friend who maybe has an addiction.

Maybe, as her best friend, I could have stopped her before things went too far.

I can't tell if my heart is sad or guilty. Probably both, wrapped in a candy coating of anger.

Mrs. Shapiro sees my face today as I walk out of homeroom, and she does more than pat me on the arm. She puts her arm around my shoulders and steers me back to her desk, in the back of the classroom.

"You okay, Evvie? You look like you're going to eat somebody."

I close my eyes. "I'm frustrated about a friend. And worried."

"Make sure you tell her those things, then."

"Good advice." Not advice I intend to take today.

"Don't let Mrs. Dearborn get you down. Concentrate on helping your friend."

Good teachers always know the score about the bad ones. I put my fist out, and she bumps it.

Today's presentations are about bison, moose, dogs,

prairie dogs, and possums, or "Please call them opossums, they're not some common animal," according to Jackie Johnson, who obviously has never seen a humble possum eating out of the barn cats' dishes in the farmyard, happy for a free meal.

The bell rings, and everyone stands up. Before I even get my backpack on my shoulder, I hear her. "Evelyn, please come up front to talk with me."

She can't have read the email already.

"Oh shit, girl, you in trouble." I hear it from behind me. "Look at Dearborn's face." I don't turn around to see who's talking.

I present myself in front of Dearborn's desk as everyone files out. "Hello, Mrs. Dearborn."

Her face is closed. "No. You may not do the octopus presentation. I don't care if you showed it to the president of the United States."

"It was a professional opportunity. It had all the requirements you asked for. It was within the time limit, it was smart, and it was funny. You didn't ask for funny." I'm digging myself a hole, but I can't help it.

"It was fine for what you needed to do, but it didn't have the intellectual sophistication a high school senior's presentation should have. Maybe you're not ready to graduate." She drills me with her eyes.

"You didn't mention sophistication in the assignment

requirements. It had extra information, and I used three- and four-syllable words. Fundraisers are plenty sophisticated. The facts were verified by Aretha's caregiver and the head Tropical Reef aquarist. Please tell me one thing that's wrong with it." I can feel the heat coming out of my ears.

"You will do your foxes presentation tomorrow if you'd like to have a grade. You have no other option."

"Then I will have completed two presentations."

"That was your choice, Evelyn. You can meet the project requirements tomorrow or not. Foxes or a zero."

"So even though I did excellent work to your specifications, plus more, it doesn't count because it was outside your torture chamber? You can't let me have my success?"

Her cheeks get a little bit red. "Why on Earth would you think I wouldn't follow my own standards? You're not some special exception." She looks down and shuffles papers on her desk. "My next class is arriving."

I turn my back on her. "I won't let you win."

"I'm the one with the power, Evvie. Your future's in my hands. Remember the stakes." She doesn't say it loud enough for the other students to hear. Just me.

"Fuck your power, you caustic bitch." I say it really low, but the sound of something knocked off her desk tells me she heard. I don't look back.

I walk out into the hall. I walk out the front door of the school. I walk to my car and drive home. When I get there, I text my mom: You have to call me in sick. I left school after Dearborn told me she had my future in her hands. Gotta work on foxes.

What a bully. Will do. I can always count on my mom to fight the power with me.

I get to work, but not until after I go outside and shatter six plates on the sidewalk—old plates, from a set we never use—and sweep up the chunks. I wrote *DEARBORN* on each one with a Sharpie. In giant letters.

Someday I'll own a business called the Break Room, a big building divided into spaces where you can throw dishes or glasses, or heavier things, like hammers, at windows. Or you can take a sledgehammer to a car. I'll make a zillion bucks, easy.

I hope all the neighbors are afraid of me now. And afraid for their dishes.

REASONS WHY ADULTS SHOULDN'T BULLY KIDS
1. THEY'RE ADULTS
2. We're kids (even if we don't think we are)
3. They have WAY more power than we do
4. THEY'RE ADULTS
5. WE'RE KIDS
6. THEY HAVE WAY MORE POWER THAN WE DO

7. You're a trash heap of a grown-up if you do it
8. Adults are supposed to help, not hurt

Blue texts me when I have a grand total of six slides and two requirements done.

PELAGIC BLUE: how was your day?

> **OCTO GIRL:** you don't want to know. fucking disaster.

PELAGIC BLUE: ?????

> **OCTO GIRL:** have to do foxes. trying to slam it together now.

PELAGIC BLUE: don't let me keep you. 😳

> **OCTO GIRL:** no, please keep me! what's new with you? how's Fishee Stixx?

I get a photo of T the DB.

> **OCTO GIRL:** beautiful as ever, i see.

PELAGIC BLUE: me and T the DB are just dreaming about Maui. freedom. relief. do u know about free diving?

OCTO GIRL: scuba diving without tanks?

PELAGIC BLUE: like they do in the water Avatar movie

OCTO GIRL: eeew yuck no colonizer movie for me thanks

PELAGIC BLUE: the nature documentary part was on point. anyway. i'm gonna learn. steady my breathing. become a fish. a dolphin. slap fins with a whale.

OCTO GIRL: you can't touch a whale!

PELAGIC BLUE: 😆😆😆😆😆😆 i would never try. you should see the whales and turtles on Maui...pure magic. i'll take you with me, if you want.

I don't answer for a second.

PELAGIC BLUE: evvie?

OCTO GIRL: how you gonna take me with you? PLUS you don't even know me. like, really know me.

PELAGIC BLUE: but i want to... I'll take you with me in my pocket. I'll send you photos and vids every day.

> **OCTO GIRL:** what if I'm a terrible, harmful human?

PELAGIC BLUE: what if you're not? what if you're just a dumbass human, like all the rest of us?

> **OCTO GIRL:** what if you're full of shit? and how you gonna slow your breath down well enough to not breathe underwater?

PELAGIC BLUE: as long as i don't think about you, i can breathe slow.

> **OCTO GIRL:** ???

PELAGIC BLUE: you make me breathe hard

> **OCTO GIRL:** omg

PELAGIC BLUE: seriously.

> **OCTO GIRL:** DO NOT SEND ME A DICK PIC

PELAGIC BLUE: i would never.

Then there's a photo of the word "DICK," written on a Post-it note.

PELAGIC BLUE: i lied.

OCTO GIRL: goofball

PELAGIC BLUE: true. so are you. i like you that way. thanks for coming on my imaginary journey

OCTO GIRL: it's my honor. if you want to take me.

PELAGIC BLUE: i want to. we can take lots of adventures.

OCTO GIRL: quest buddies. adventure pals.

PELAGIC BLUE: that's us. OH. speaking of adventures, i don't think Fishee Stixx will want a plane adventure. will you keep Terrence for me while i'm gone?

OCTO GIRL: does Fishee have a lid for her tank? remember, i have a cat?

PELAGIC BLUE: yes, T the DB has a lid on his tank.

OCTO GIRL: then of course. i'd be honored to keep Fishee for you.

PELAGIC BLUE: thank you a million.

OCTO GIRL:

PELAGIC BLUE: now get your ass to work and get it done. we have missions to go on. journeys. escapades.

OCTO GIRL: on it. thank you.

PELAGIC BLUE: my honor.

Oh wow. I'm an adventure buddy now.

I feel the happiness bursting out of the top of my head.

It powers the rest of my night.

21

BY MORNING, I'VE GOT DEARBORN'S REQUIREMENTS COMPLETE. MY MOM GETS UP EARLY and helps me polish the whole thing. It's not as good as Aretha's presentation, but it's more than decent. It's a solid B.

REASONS WHY FOXES AREN'T NEARLY AS COOL AS OCTOPUSES

1. They live in forests, grasslands, mountains, deserts, and urban areas.
   a. None of which are the ocean.
2. They have fur.
   a. Fur is common.
   b. Octopuses have chromatophores.
   c. FWOOSH.

3. Foxes, at their biggest, weigh thirty-ish
   pounds.
   a. The giant Pacific octopus can
      weigh up to six hundred pounds.
   b. An octopus with eight-foot arms is
      another level of cuddling.

I'm too tired to get to eight.

The one legitimately cooler thing a red fox has over an octopus is its scientific name: *Vulpes vulpes*. Mysterious and exotic. *Octopus cyanea* isn't as sexy as *Vulpes vulpes*.

I text Lucie: Dearborn's making me do foxes. Aretha forever!

Lucie sends back a ton of angry faces and two sentences: GRADUATE SO YOU CAN COME WORK WITH US. Done is good!

A fair point.

I do my presentation when Dearborn calls my name. It's fine. She nods in a couple places, and she claps when I'm done, just like everyone else does. I'm second to last for the day.

My body starts to relax when I'm finally back in my desk, and by the time class is over, I'm a limp noodle. I skip a few classes for a nap in the Lair, but I finish the day strong.

She cannot defeat me. I will not let her.

After school, I text Ken. I've thought a lot about what to say, but I'm tired, so it all just comes out: please get help. i'm not good at being friends with high or drunk Ken. i don't know if this is addiction or not, and i'm eternally sorry for my part in it, and I'll help you get out of it, but I don't like you like this. i'm scared for you, and i want you to have a future. i needed that video, and you couldn't help me. i'm still pissed. but i love you and want the best for you.

Not eloquent, but honest.

Dearborn claims to be holding my future in her hands.

Ken has her future in her hands but is trashing it.

Which is worse?

22

THE DAY AFTER AN ALL-NIGHTER IS WORSE FOR ME, SO I DRIFT OFF IN DEAR-born's class, where two kids are finishing up their presentations—bats and mice, and the bat one was pretty interesting—which results in Dearborn asking the kid next to me to slam his book on my desk to wake me up, which he does, and I jump a thousand miles and almost punch him, and everyone laughs.

Then Dearborn tells me to come back after school.

In all my other classes, I do everything I'm asked to do, hoping that the good vibes will extend to Dearborn so she will see she's truly wrong and I truly just need to graduate.

I can't eat lunch. I sit in the Lair and tap my foot

until Gus Gus tells me he's going to cut my foot off if I don't stop, which are big words from him. I tuck my foot underneath me.

I'm too embarrassed to tell Rachel I had to do foxes.

How could I ever have thought Dearborn would change? Zebras don't change their stripes, to use a mammal analogy. I can imagine almost anything to be true, even when it's not.

Dearborn has zero capacity to be anything but herself: a rigid, self-righteous bitch.

Why would I rationally think there are other possibilities?

I hate this brain. Hate it.

After school, I go to Dearborn's room. On Fridays, teachers get to go home right away, so she's standing behind her desk, packed up and ready to leave, purse over one arm and homework in a bag over the other. She looks calm and cool. My insides, on the other hand, are some unholy cross between a cheetah and a sloth.

"You wanted to see me?" I put on a polite face.

"I've graded your foxes presentation, and you're two points shy of a passing grade. You won't be graduating."

"I'm...what?"

She says it again, slower and louder, like I've lost my hearing and my wits. Which I have. "You will not be graduating. You will need to take this class during summer school."

"Will...will you be teaching it?"

"No." She looks like she wants to spit at me. "I don't want to see you again."

I can't think of a single thing to say.

"I told you your future was in my hands, Evvie. The stakes are higher than you can imagine if you don't graduate. So I suggest you shape up for summer school."

She can't be this mean. "Is there anything I can do to get those two points back?" I can barely talk.

"No." I swear her eyeballs are little flickering fires, like she's the devil herself.

"Mrs. Dearborn—"

"No. We're done." And she walks around her desk, walks by me, and walks out her door. I stare after her.

She can't really do that, can she?

I did two presentations and followed all the requirements for both.

Two points?

Rachel will know. I have to get to the Lair before I burst into tears.

I barely get my key in the door. "RACHEL! Are you here? Rachel?" The door to the band room is shut. I open it and holler again. "RACHEL!"

She comes out of her office with wide eyes. "What the flip is wrong with you?"

"DEARBOOOOOOOORN!" I flop on the couch. Through my tears, I notice a sign on the back of the door I just came in: TURN IN YOUR KEYS TO RACHEL BY THE LAST DAY OF THE SCHOOL YEAR. THIS MEANS YOU: GUS GUS, EVVIE, ROSE.

I can't process that right now.

Rachel's made it into the Lair by this point. "Dearborn what?"

"Dearborn just told me I'm not going to pass Biology. By two points. There's nothing I can do." I'm wailing.

Rachel pulls me onto my feet and into a hug. "We'll figure it out."

"How the FUCK are we going to do that?"

"I don't know. Maybe the superintendent. Maybe we can talk Dearborn down. You did two reports, which is more than other people did. I heard your Aretha one was perfect."

"How did…"

"Sam. He got the link from Rose, after she asked you for it. He also said you should talk for a living. You're very persuasive."

I snort.

"Even if the foxes one was bad, the combination should be more than a passing grade. We'll figure it out, okay?"

She's pat-pat-patting my back, and I've got my head on her shoulder. I'm looking out the window, trying to get my eyes to focus through the tears.

And when they do, I see Gus Gus on the bench. Reading and waiting for a ride home.

It's an ordinary spring day, sunny and bright, with green grass and trees, and Gus Gus is reading outside.

A new red pickup truck pulls up really close to the bench.

The passenger window opens.

Gus Gus doesn't notice at all.

Fire comes out the window of the truck. And lands on Gus Gus.

I see the tip of something stick out the window.

Then, somehow, the fire turns into a fireball.

And the truck drives away.

One beat of silence, while my brain registers what happened.

"GUS GUS! GUS GUS!" All I can do is scream and point.

Rachel pulls away, looks at me, looks where I'm pointing, then vaults the couch, opens the window that nobody knew could open until two weeks ago, shoves the screen out, jumps, and runs.

I'm right behind her.

Gus Gus isn't making a sound. He's just trying to pat the fire out with his hands.

Rachel strips off her shirt and smothers him as she pulls him off the bench. She wraps his torso with her arms and the fabric while he stands frozen in shock.

I look down the street, and the truck is barreling around a corner. It's too far away to get the plate. But I can guess who owns it.

"Gus Gus! Talk to us!" Rachel wipes at Gus Gus's face with her shirt. The tank top she's wearing is covered in soot, as is Gus Gus's face. "Call 911, Evvie. Now."

"I was on fire." Gus Gus holds up the palms of his hands, which are angry and red. There are blisters on his face and on his neck. His shirt is partially burned away.

"Who was that, Gus Gus?" I'm so furious I'm shaking.

Rachel moves to stomp on Gus Gus's book because it's on fire, too.

"I was reading my book, and then I was on fire. Something landed in my lap. Then it exploded. I need to sit." Gus Gus crumples back onto the bench.

We look around. A white rag is smoldering by the side of the bench. Rachel stomps on it, too. Then she kneels in front of Gus Gus, looking him over. "Was it hard, the thing that hit you?"

"Soft. I was reading." Gus Gus closes his eyes.

"Hang on, friend. Hang on." I rush behind the bench and hold Gus Gus's shoulders, because I have no idea what else to do. "Hang on. We're here."

I have to do something.

What if he dies?

He won't die. His burns aren't that bad.

But what if I'm wrong?

That complete motherfucker.

Rachel looks at me "EVVIE. Do you have your phone?"

I pat my pants pocket, leaving my other hand on Gus Gus's shoulder. "Yes."

"Call 911, then call the office and tell them to call Gus Gus's mom. Tell them to tell her to meet us at the hospital. We've got to get these burns checked." She picks her shirt up from the ground, shakes it out, puts it on, then sits down next to Gus Gus. He tilts onto her shoulder, and she slides her arm around him. "It's okay, Gus Gus. We'll make it okay as soon as we can. It's okay, sweetheart." She pats his leg with the hand that's not on his shoulder and keeps crooning. "Let's get you to the hospital, sweetheart. Your mom will find us there. Were you waiting for her?"

"I don't drive." Gus Gus has his eyes closed, leaning on Rachel.

"MAKE THAT CALL, EVVIE." Rachel snaps me out of my anger. "Then go back in through the window and get my purse. Hurry." Her eyes are as frightened as I feel, but her voice is steady.

I run back toward the building, dialing 911. I give

them the info, and they promise it will be quick. Before I can find the office phone number in my phone, I hear the ambulance siren.

They're gonna have to take him to Chaska. We don't have a hospital here.

When Marta, the admin assistant, answers, it's all I can do not to scream *VANDAL MCDANIEL JUST LIT GUS GUS ON FIRE.* I take a deep breath and lean on the building. "Marta, Gus Gus Snyder just got injured. Can you call his mom? Ms. Brownlee is waiting with him for the ambulance, and she'll follow behind in her car. His mom can meet them in Chaska."

Marta gasps. "But...Rachel needs permission to accompany a student in an emergency!"

"I think his mom will forgive Rachel. Can you please just do it? He's hurt bad."

Marta tsk-tsks into the phone. "Next time make sure she fills out the form."

"SOMEONE LIT THE MAN ON FIRE AND THIS IS NOT THE TIME FOR FORMS." I hang up on her and climb through the window.

Thank god Rachel left her office door open. I grab her purse and run back to the bench.

The ambulance is just pulling up. Gus Gus is panting a bit and crying, but not a lot. Rachel's soothing him like he's three.

"Does it hurt, Gus Gus?" I don't know what else to say.

He nods.

The very efficient paramedics have him on a stretcher in no time flat, and Rachel takes off running to her car, purse flying behind her, once she's sure they're going to Chaska.

"I love you, Gus Gus." I bend in and kiss him on the shoulder, since his cheek is starting to blister. I'm crying, Rachel was crying when she ran for her car, I'm sure Gus Gus's mom is crying by now, and the paramedics keep being efficient. Gus Gus is ashy gray, and his eyes are closed. They lift him into the back, shut the doors, and speed away. I watch Rachel peel out of the parking lot to follow behind them, and then I seriously cannot think what the fuck to do next.

I walk back to the building, slower than anybody's grandma, and climb back in through the window. I shut Rachel's office door, and I make sure the Lair is locked. I am deliberate in my actions so I don't forget anything.

Then I walk to my locker, get my backpack, walk outside and put the screen back in the window, walk to my car, and get in.

Then I sit there. If I move, I'll fall apart.

I'm not graduating. Dearborn said so.

But that anger has just been eclipsed.

The only person I can think of who might be able to help is Mr. Dawson, our superintendent. By now, both Dawson and Garfield will know about what happened to Gus Gus, thanks to Marta, but Garfield won't do anything to the son of an old drinking buddy.

Dawson lives down the street from me.

When I get home, it's four thirty, and it's still too early to feed Popcorn, but I do it, because my mom's got a meeting tonight with her thesis advisor and won't be home until late. I leave her a note: *Bad day today. trying to make it better. i'm safe and okay. See you soon. XXXOOO*

Then I plant my ass on Bob Dawson's front step and wait for him to get home.

Robert Dawson is an all right guy, but he's still a guy, a middle-aged one, and probably a neurotypical guy. I don't generally trust guys like him. He has kids who are younger than me, and they used to live here, too, until he and his wife got a divorce. The kids are in middle school by now, I'd think.

I sit. I look at my phone. I text Sam and Rose so they'll know what's happened. I think about texting Ken, but I don't.

I text Blue: i'm not graduating, and someone lit my friend Gus Gus on fire. Pretty sure this is the end times.

His reply is instantaneous: you're not graduating?

OCTO GIRL: not at this point.
BUT SOMEONE LIT MY FRIEND
ON FIRE. that's just fucked up.

PELAGIC BLUE: no words for that.

Then I message Rachel: HOW IS GUS GUS??
It's 5:20 and Bob Dawson still isn't home.

I contemplate going to Vandal's farm to see if the truck is there. I contemplate going to the cop shop. I contemplate how hungry I am.

Can Dearborn really do that? Keep me from graduating because of two points?

Is revenge on a student her ultimate pedagogical goal?

Do I want to know the answer to that?

I close my eyes. My heart turns into Minnesota granite.

My phone vibrates, and I snatch it up. It's Rachel.

RACHEL: Gus Gus will be okay. Burns
are mostly first-degree, with a few
second-degree spots. He went home
with his mom, and I'm home now, too.

EVVIE: Oh thank god. Thank you,
Jesus and Mary and Buddha and
Krishna and Yahweh and Guan Yin
and Pele and Kali.

RACHEL: How do you know all those deities?

EVVIE: Long story.

She doesn't know about my religious hyperfixation in eighth grade.

RACHEL: Don't even think about going after Vandal. We have to do this right. The cops were at the hospital, and they have a description of the pickup, best as Gus Gus could give them.

EVVIE: Vandal's been after us all semester.

RACHEL: We have to be able to prove it was him. I'm working on that.

EVVIE: He takes what he wants. He's a motherfucker. Gus Gus is right.

RACHEL: What are you doing right now?

At that moment, Robert Dawson pulls into his driveway with a quizzical look for me.

EVVIE: Nothing. Gotta go!

I shove my phone into my backpack.

Mr. Dawson gets out of his car and gives me a look. "May I help you, Evvie?"

"I sure do hope so." I don't smile. "As you may already know, one of our BLAHS students was lit on fire today by another BLAHS student. First of all, that student needs to be arrested, because it's assault. Secondly, the fire starter is a graduation speaker, and now that he's lit a fellow senior on fire, I don't believe he should be given the honor of speaking. How are you going to fix this?"

Dawson looks at me, heaves his shoulders up in a big sigh, and drops his briefcase next to me on the front steps. "Evvie. You have no idea who did this. Gus Gus isn't sure who did this."

"I am one hundred percent certain it was Vandal McDaniel. He's been after the kids who"—I almost say *hang out in the Lair*, but I don't know what Dawson knows about the Lair—"aren't like him since Gus Gus called him a motherfucker a few weeks ago." Mr. Dawson winces at the word. "Nobody has any reason to hate on Gus Gus. Vandal's got it in his head that it's his right to bust Gus Gus down, and now he's lit him on fire. So what will you do?"

Mr. Robert Dawson, the most powerful man in BLAS, looks at me. Just looks. "Evvie."

"You know Vandal is the most likely culprit. You've

been the superintendent since Vandal and I were in middle school. You know what he does."

He sighs again. "I do. I'm also aware of the influence his family has in this town."

I stand straight up. "You're telling me you're not going to do anything about this? Because of Vandal's DAD?"

"I'm telling you I can't do anything about it until we know who hurt Gus Gus. If we can make a definite identification of the culprit, and it's Vandal, then the police will do something. I'll do something. I can't do it on just your word."

"Mr. Dawson, were you a football player in high school?"

His forehead wrinkles up. "What does that have to do with anything?"

"Were you, Mr. Dawson?"

"I was, actually. I played for Holy Angels." It's a private school in the Cities that always has a good football team.

"Did you pick on the geeks? The weirdos? The nerds? The kids who were just a little different?"

I see a shadow cross his face.

"Tell me, Mr. Dawson. Did you?"

"I don't know if I want to answer that." His smile is uncomfortable, so that's enough answer for me.

"I'm asking you to think about those kids right now. Those kids you hated on and ignored in high school.

Gus Gus is one of those kids, and Vandal is a kid like you were. Do you endorse what Vandal did?"

Another shadow crosses his face.

"Think about it, Mr. Dawson. Think about it hard." I pick up my backpack. "Which side of history are you gonna stand on? Are you gonna enable Vandal's shitty behavior or confront it? Are you gonna keep repping for the jocks, preps, and socials? Or are you gonna come in clutch for the weirdos and the regular kids?"

It feels risky to lay slang on a grown-up, but my adult language seems to have deserted me.

He closes his eyes, sighs again, then opens them. His shoulders are slumped, but his smile is a little bit kind. "Can I go in now, Evvie? It's been a bit of a day. Thank you for expressing your concerns." His tone isn't mean or rude. It's just tired.

"Thank you for listening, Mr. Dawson." I walk to my car. The house door shuts behind me.

Once I get in, I message Rachel again: There's a school board meeting before graduation, right? To firm up plans? Please tell me this is right.

RACHEL: In a couple days. Why?

EVVIE: I've got that many days
to get evidence that Vandal was

EVVIE: Gus Gus's attacker, and
I've got to bring it to Bob Dawson.
Can you help me with this??

RACHEL: Evvie, what are you doing??

EVVIE: Can you help me, Rachel?

RACHEL: 😊😊😊😊😊 I will help you.
But you gotta let the system work.

EVVIE: Since when has the system
ever worked for people like Gus Gus?

RACHEL: Fair point. Now go home
and eat supper. Tell your mom about
Dearborn. Work on solving that
problem, because it's more immediate.
Gus Gus is gonna be okay.

EVVIE: I will strip naked if Vandal is
a graduation speaker, and nobody
wants that, so letting this go is a big
ol' negatory, ten-four, over and out.

RACHEL: I hear you, honey. I hear you.

I drive out to Vandal's farm. Everyone already knows
where it is, but all the super-nice stuff is a dead giveaway.

There's a swimming pool, and a dirt track for racing motorized go-karts, plus all the regular farm stuff. You can't miss it.

I drive by, really slowly, and I see the red pickup. Ha ha, dipshit. I got you now. And then I see another pickup just like it. And then a third just like it. Evidently, farm corporations like a uniform look?

What if the cops look in the wrong one? What can I do to make sure they have the right one?

Asshole!

I'm so pissed, I flip a U right in the middle of the highway, and people honk and honk. I speed back into town and drive around the whole perimeter three times, thinking about how to get Vandal's ass to the cops. When I drive by the grocery store, I see two more trucks that look just like the ones in Vandal's farmyard.

Why are red pickups so popular in Bluestem Lake?

GODDAMN IT.

I go home. It's seven by now, and I'm hungry. But once I get there, I can't do anything but sit on the couch. I can't make myself supper, I can't turn on the lights, I can't go pee. I'm just stuck, thinking about Gus Gus and Dearborn. They chase themselves in my head.

About nine thirty, the lock unlocks and my mom walks in. She stops when she sees the dark room "Evvie? Are you here?"

"Right here." My voice is small.

She turns on a light. "Why are you sitting in the dark?"

"Because today was a mess. Because today I learned about stakes."

She pulls up the footstool, sits in front of me, and takes my hands. "What happened?"

"Gus Gus got lit on fire by Vandal, and Dearborn told me I couldn't graduate. I'm two points short to pass her class."

Her eyes go wide. "Is Gus Gus okay?"

"I think so. At least that's what Rachel said. He got to go home. No skin grafts."

"Thank heavens! Did you see it happen?"

I nod.

She's looking me over, almost like she's checking for injuries. "Are you okay? Did they arrest Vandal?" She remembers Vandal from middle school.

"I don't think so. And that's what's making me maddest."

"Let the cops handle that part, okay?" She squeezes my hands. "Now tell me about the other part. You can't graduate?"

"It's more important that Gus Gus got lit on fire, Mom."

She moves from the footstool to the couch and gathers

me in her arms. "You're right, but Gus Gus has a mom to worry about him. You don't have to do it right now. I'm the mom who gets to worry about you."

"Life is too overwhelming. I can't do it."

"I know, my love. I know."

I burst into tears.

We sit like that for a very, very long time.

REASONS WHY THE WORLD IS HORRIBLE
1. People like Vandal McDaniel
2. People like Audrey Dearborn
3. People who litter and/or pollute
4. People who abuse others in any way: physical, verbal, emotional, sexual, all of it
5. People who hurt children in any way: physically, sexually, mentally, emotionally, spiritually, *any way at all*
6. People who abuse power
7. People
8. People like Vandal

Fuck you, Vandal.

23

ON MONDAY, I DON'T COME OUT OF THE LAIR. I GO TO HOMEROOM, BUT I CAN'T make myself go to Dearborn's class, or any other one. Besides, if Dearborn's not passing me, then fuck school, and if Gus Gus is so expendable that SOME-ONE CAN SET HIM ON FIRE, what's the point of any of it?

I sit in Gus Gus's squishy armchair and take turns staring at my phone and staring out the window—lucky for me, the chair swivels. I eat six CLIF Bars, which becomes grossly unhealthy after a while, but my brain is mush. Rachel sticks her head in the door from the band room every so often—she's worried. Rose, Sam, Sagal, and three students I don't know are in and out all day, all of them shooting their concerned eyes at me, but I don't talk to anyone.

Gus Gus texts me close to last period: Will you come see me?

Of course. I stand up, grab my backpack, and open the window.

"Holy shit, all of my dreams have just come true!" Sam arrives at the right time to fulfill his best school fantasies. I nod, exit not very gracefully, and walk across the lawn to the student parking lot.

I'm sure Rachel won't be pleased, but whatever. Times are desperate and hard.

Gus Gus's house is on the opposite side of town from mine, and even though Bluestem Lake is small, I don't get to his corner of the world very often. You could probably put three of my houses in his.

His tiny and shy mom answers the enormous door, which is at the end of an enormous sidewalk that branches from the enormous driveway. She points me to an enormous and all-cream living room without really looking at me. Gus Gus is the only spot of color in there.

How do people live like this? Too big. Too perfect.

Gus Gus has bandages on his chin and along his jawbone, creeping up his cheeks a bit. There's also a big bandage on his chest—he's got on a bathrobe rather than a shirt. His eyes get happy when he sees me, and he tries to smile, but I can see it hurts.

"Can you talk? Does it hurt your face too much?" I am immediately crying, even though I don't want to be.

He shakes his head and points to a pad of paper and a Sharpie.

"Is there something I can do for you? I'm on it, whatever it is. I'm so angry, Gus Gus." I wipe the tears, and my nose, with my sleeve. Gus Gus hands me a box of Kleenex as he nods.

I blow my nose while he writes. It's obvious his writing hand hurts a lot by the way he's holding the Sharpie, but neither hand has bandages.

It's just one sentence: *YOU HAVE TO GO AFTER DEARBORN.*

"How do you know about that?"

He writes more: *RACHEL WAS ON HER PHONE IN THE EMERGENCY ROOM. DON'T KNOW WITH WHO. SHE SAID YOU'RE NOT GRADUATING.*

"Yeah, well, Vandal lit you on fire. That's way more bullshit than me not graduating. I can take a summer class. I'm clueless about my future, anyway, so no big loss."

Gus Gus writes again: *THE POLICE WILL FIND VANDAL. DEARBORN'S A BIGGER SLIMEBUCKET. YOU DID TWO PRESENTATIONS, AND EVERYONE ELSE DID ONE. GO AFTER HER.*

Slimebucket. That makes me smile. "My foxes presentation wasn't as good as my Aretha one, and that's what she graded."

YOU STILL DID TWO, ONE AS AN EXPERT AND A PROFESSIONAL. ONE WAS BRILLIANT, ONE WAS PASSABLE. He pauses to massage his hand.

"I have no power. She told me so herself." I feel the tears starting up again.

He shakes his head. *THERE'S GOT TO BE A WAY. CAN'T DAWSON DO SOMETHING?*

It didn't even occur to me to mention Dearborn to him last night. "Maybe. I don't know. I don't know if I trust him."

Gus Gus looks at me, then writes. *YOU'VE GOT TO TRUST ANOTHER GROWN-UP BESIDES RACHEL.*

"There's zero reason to trust anyone besides Rachel. And T. And Carl the Custodian. And my mom. That's enough."

Gus Gus sighs and looks sad. Then he writes. *YOU WORKED TOO HARD TO GIVE UP NOW. YOU DID YOUR SOPHOMORE AND JUNIOR YEAR AT THE SAME TIME. THIS WAS YOUR LAST HURDLE. DON'T LET HER KEEP YOU FROM JUMPING OVER THAT BASTARD AND CROSSING THE FINISH LINE.*

He puts the pad and Sharpie down and leans back

against the couch. He's said more in the last few minutes than he's said in the last two months. Gus Gus closes his eyes. His face is moving into that ashy-gray color from Friday.

"You okay?"

He nods.

"I'm sorry that tired you out."

Gus Gus waves his nonwriting hand but doesn't open his eyes.

"You gonna walk at graduation, with all your bandages?"

His eyes fly open, then get hard and steely, and he nods as he picks up the pad again. *VANDAL CAN'T SCARE ME, AND DEARBORN CAN'T SCARE YOU. FUCK THAT SHIT.* Then he rips off all the pages of his pad that he's written on—which is very hard to do when your hands are burned, but he gets it done—and hands them to me.

"Don't want your mom to see you cussing?" I smile.

He nods and leans back on the couch, closing his eyes again.

"Need some water? A snack? Anything? I bet you can't eat in this room, though, can you?"

He smiles a tiny bit, eyes still closed, and gives me a thumbs-up.

His mom comes to look in on us. "Can I get you

anything…I don't know your name." Her smile is hesitant but still kind. "I know Gus Gus doesn't hang out with many people."

"I'm Evvie, and no, thank you, I'm fine. But I think Gus Gus could use some water."

Another thumbs-up from the couch. She nods and turns around.

"Is your mom shy?"

He moves his nonwriting hand in a *so-so* way.

"Is she like you?"

Thumbs-up.

"How about your dad?"

Thumbs-up.

"Do you have any siblings?"

Thumbs-down.

"Your dad made all his money in tech, I'm betting."

Double thumbs-up.

"Stereotypes for the win." I pat Gus Gus's knee. "I'm gonna scram and talk to my mom. And Rachel. Maybe they have ideas for how to make a dent in Dearborn."

Very tired-looking thumbs-up.

I bend over him and kiss his cheek where it's not bandaged. "You're my favorite, Gus Gus. You really are."

He nods.

I slip out of the house before his mom comes back with the water.

*   *   *

How do you walk around after someone lights you on fire? How do you trust anyone, especially in public? How do you calm your brain down?

Maybe Gus Gus's brain won't internalize it.

Mine already did, and it didn't even happen to me.

When I get home, my mom studies me. "Why are your eyes red?"

"I saw Gus Gus." The tears are threatening again.

"Oh, my love." She gathers me in her arms and hugs me tight.

"He's gonna be fine, I think. He's got bandages on his chest, chin, and jaw. They look scary." I say it to her shoulder. "When we stand up for ourselves, why are people such fuckwads?"

She laughs and pulls back from me so I can see her face. "Difference is threatening. Besides that, Vandal is afraid Gus Gus is right about him—then he'd have to admit to himself that he's an asshole. And Vandal can't handle that."

"The cops have to arrest him."

"Hopefully those wheels are in motion. Gus Gus went to the hospital, so the medical staff will corroborate that it's assault. And I'm sure Rachel's doing all she can. But you, my love, have to think about Dearborn."

"Why?" I slump my ass onto a kitchen chair. "She's Audrey Dearborn, hater of Evelyn Chambers, and she has the power. She controls my future, remember, and when has anyone stopped a teacher who hates a student? Never."

"Hate? Really?" My mom sits down across from me at the table.

"She hates me because I don't believe her bullshit that I need to change."

My mom rolls her eyes, but her smile is huge. "Obviously my parenting strategy of loving you extra hard has succeeded extra well." She laughs. "Of course you don't need to change. But let's talk about choices. You can decide to work within the system that's established, or you can exit the system." She levels a look at me.

"So you're saying changing the system is too hard?"

"I'm saying the system is the system, and you can change it, but first you have to get what you need from the system." She raises her eyebrows. "Are you picking up what I'm putting down?"

I think for a second. "You're saying I need to graduate."

"I feel confident you'll go to college after your gap year—even if your gap year is a couple years long—and you can't do that without a high school diploma. I also feel confident you can get a better job before you go to college if you have a high school diploma."

"Getting a GED can't be that hard."

"But you'll have to study for it, to review all the things you forgot, and that will piss you off, so you'll quit studying, and then you won't have a GED or a high school diploma. If you talk to Dearborn, maybe there's something you can do right now to make it better. Avoid the other hassle."

"She's a fucking bitch." I say it while looking my mom straight in the face.

"That may be, but she's who you've got to work with right now. So figure it out. Or don't. The choice is yours." She sits back in the chair, daring me to disagree. "Never let anyone say you need to change. Just learn how to play their game."

"How do I do that after she's declared there's no more game?"

"Be nice and kiss her ass. Send an email and ask her what extra work you can do. Who cares what she thinks of you? You're walking away into a better life—one you can design for yourself—and she'll still be here, small-minded and stuck in Bluestem Lake. You'll still graduate, whether it's now or at the end of the summer, and you'll be out of there. You control your future, not her."

I can't argue with that. "What do I say in the email?"

My mom laughs. "Pretend you want something from me, and I'm being particularly difficult about it. What would you say to me?"

"I'd butter you up by reminding you that I'm your favorite child and the most wonderful child you've ever met, and that you love me more than you love yourself, because you've told me that for my entire life. I can't say that to her."

"No, but you can remind her of all the good things you've done, and all the effort you've put in. Sending an email is also creating documentation, in case we have to take this to another level."

"Do we need to do that?"

She sighs. "I don't know yet. Her reaction is unreasonable. She's withholding two measly points in an arbitrary scale that doesn't mean anything anyway."

"Excuse me?" No grown-up in my life has ever said grades don't mean anything.

"Grades mostly measure how well a person follows directions and standards, and they may or may not be good directions and standards to begin with. Grades are rarely useful except to measure obedience."

"Gotcha." I'm slightly blown away, but duh.

"I will never, ever, ever keep a student from something they need. Fuck power trips." She is dead serious. "Right now, though, you don't have to defeat all the terrible people. You just have to care for yourself in the face of them and get what you need from them."

BINGO.

My brain suddenly rights itself, and the ship is back on course.

I stand up. "I get it. I'm on it." I go around the table to hug her. "Thanks for being so smart."

She hugs me back. "I'm trying to teach you all the stuff no one ever taught me."

I give her one more squeeze, then go to grab a frozen pizza. My mom settles on the couch with the work she has to do tonight. When the pizza is done, we eat it together in the living room. Then I go to my room and open my computer.

I put on a song that makes me feel really strong: "Fight the Power" by Public Enemy, which was absolutely not written for a white girl in Minnesota, but here we are. Thank you, Public Enemy.

The course management system actually says "BLAS-BLAHS" at the top of its home page. What I'm about to write is some serious blah-blah.

I open an email to Dearborn.

I put on my camouflage. FWOOSH.

It takes me ninety minutes.

Dear Mrs. Dearborn:

When the aquarium keepers asked me to do the presentation for the fundraisers, my goal was to showcase what kind of excellent animal Aretha is, and how she can be an asset for fundraising. It also gave me practice for my foxes presentation. As you know, I was also hopeful you might consent to counting the octopus presentation for my grade instead of the foxes, but that was your call. I understand I didn't put the same amount of work into my foxes presentation, and that's on me.

Is there anything I can do to make up the two points I need to pass your class? I passed the final exam with an 85 percent. Can doing two presentations instead of one (one excellent, one average) count for two more points? I will do any assignment you'd like. Please help me achieve my goal of graduating high school. As you know, my sophomore year was difficult, and I've worked very hard to make up the time I lost that year. Please help me finish what I've started.

I hope to hear from you. Thank you for your time.

Sincerely,
Evvie

Here's what I want to write: You're a grown-up. Why is your ego more important than my future? Why are you so hateful?

The word "hate" is harsh and ugly. I'll drop the f-bomb sixty hundred times in terrible contexts with inappropriate audiences before I'll enjoy using the word "hate."

Do humans get more ridiculous as we get older? Meaner? More insecure? What is it?

AAAAAAAAAAAAAAAAAAAAAAAAAAAAAAAH.

I shut my computer and go back to the living room. My mom is sleeping on the couch, books open in her lap. I move the books to the coffee table and find a blanket to cover her with, then give her a kiss on the forehead when I'm done. She doesn't move.

Popcorn wants to know what I'm doing, but I don't let her come into the backyard with me.

I'm trying to get a better perspective on the shit show that is my life, kitty. That's what I'm doing.

THINGS THAT ARE GOOD ABOUT THE WORLD

1. Nature, when we don't ruin it
   a. Minnesota has awesome nature
   b. Lake Superior, forests, waterfalls, prairies, regular lakes, rivers, Minnesota animals like lynx and bears and eagles and yeah. Good nature here.

2. Animals—Popcorn, Aretha, foxes, all of them
   a. Insects, too
   b. Anything alive that moves—
      excluding Vandal and Dearborn
3. Dessert
   a. Any kind except pudding
   b. Though I do love crème brûlée, and
      that's a custard
4. Kissing
   a. Especially when you understand it
      a bit better
   b. And have someone to do it with
5. Spring—the FUCKING BEST. Omg
6. Chances to pivot
7. Darkness
   a. But also light
   b. Gotta have one to have the other
8. Vibing and peacing out—as in relaxing to
   enjoy some peace, not leaving
   a. Even though I generally suck at relaxing
   b. Aaaauuuummmm
   c. Breathe iiiiiiiiiiiiiiiiiiiiin
   d. Breathe ouuuuuuuuuuuut

It's cool and nice outside. May's one of my favorite months. I take a lawn chair from the garage, park it in the middle of the yard, and take off my Birks. Under my naked feet, there's a vibration moving through the dirt. It comes up through my soles, through my body, and out the top of my head. It connects me to the cosmos Gus Gus was reading about.

It's good to be reminded there are forces much bigger than you at work in the world.

Forces that don't care how you think or feel.

Forces that include you in their movement simply because you're alive.

24

WHEN I GET IN MY CAR TO LEAVE FOR SCHOOL, I FIND A POST-IT NOTE ON the steering wheel: *RESPECT EXISTENCE OR EXPECT RESISTANCE. I LOVE YOU! MOM*

Nice one. I stick it on the crappy radio I never use. Aux cord all the way, baby.

Gus Gus isn't back at school, but he barely had classes, anyway. Rose and Sam are in the Lair before homeroom with a box of doughnuts. Rose hands it to me. "Want one?"

"Sure." I take a chocolate doughnut with chocolate glaze. "Where'd they come from?"

"We found them in here with a note that said *RESPECT EXISTENCE OR EXPECT RESISTANCE.*

Must be Rachel?" Rose takes a big bite of her glazed doughnut.

"Must be." I take a bite, too. "But after the deer-piss incident, should we really be eating them?"

Rose's eyes get huge. But she swallows, anyway.

Do my mom and Rachel know each other?

This town is so damn small.

Or maybe the Universe is just that mysterious.

In homeroom, I ask Mrs. Shapiro if I can just sit in the corner of the room for the rest of the day. She says no, the year's almost done, I should go to the rest of my classes. But she's really kind when she says it. She pats my shoulder when I leave.

FWOOSH. I put on as much camouflage as I can think of on the way to Dearborn's class.

Because everything's done for the semester, we play name that organ, in teams, and my team wins—big—but Dearborn says there's no prize. Nobody likes this fact, and there are rumbles from the teams.

"Mrs. Dearborn, why not?" A very smart sophomore named Edel Martinez seems quite concerned by this reversal of fortune.

"Your grades are already figured, so there's no need. It's just extra work for me."

More rumbles from the crowd. I hear Edel say to his

buddy, "It's just clicking a button." Dearborn hears him, but she smiles like she didn't, like everything is fine.

I have to physically restrain my arm from shooting out of its socket and physically stifle my voice from saying, *If you gave me the bonus points you normally give for this game, I'd pass and graduate, and you can't have that, can you?*

I blink and camouflage until the bell rings. It could've been three minutes or three years.

Everyone's filing out, and I approach her desk. She's looking at me like she's ready for battle. FWOOSH. My camouflage is tight.

"Did you read my email, Mrs. Dearborn? Is there something I can do to make my grade better? My team won name that organ today. If you give me the traditional five bonus points you normally give to name-that-organ winners, the situation would be solved." I smile, not too big, not too forcefully, simply and calmly, as if I always stick up for myself in front of adult bullies.

Dearborn stares right into my eyes. "My mind is made up, Evelyn. You will not pass this class. You can do nothing." She folds her arms.

"This decision is fickle, arbitrary, and educationally backward." I turn around to leave.

She snorts. "Everyone knows what kind of trouble-maker you are."

I go straight to the office. I'm not angry-crying, for once, and I'm glad.

Marta's on the phone, and she looks concerned. There's a police officer sitting in one of the chairs people sit in while they wait to be banished to the Hole. He looks bored. The door to Mr. Dawson's office is open, but the door to the conference room off the main office is closed.

I stand there like I belong there. I'm shaking like I just ran ten miles.

Marta hangs up the phone and gives me the stink eye. "Can I help you, Evvie?"

"I'd like to see Mr. Dawson, please."

She gestures to the closed door. "He's meeting with the school board right now, talking about graduation. And you can see we have bigger things going on." She gestures to the police officer, who nods and goes back to his phone. "Does your problem truly require his attention?"

"It certainly does. It's probably wise to talk with the school board, too." I march forward, walk around Marta's desk, and open the door to the conference room like I was invited.

"Evelyn Chambers!" Marta stands up, ready to come after me.

In front of me are Mr. Dawson, a woman I don't know, a man I don't know, and Rose's mom, Beth.

"Good morning, school board and Mr. Dawson. Could I please have a moment of your time?" I mentally check my camouflage, then give them my very best angry face. "I'd like you to be aware of two different academic injustices that are part of graduation."

"Evelyn!" Marta isn't giving up.

Mr. Dawson looks at my face and then at the school board members, who can see I'm distressed. "It's fine, Marta. We've got ten minutes for Evvie."

"Thank you." I shut the door behind me, in Marta's face, but not before I notice her frown and smile back at her.

When I turn to the school board members, the two I don't know seem annoyed by the interruption. Mr. Dawson looks resigned.

Rose's mom, Beth, looks curious. "What's up, Evvie? What's happened?" She gestures to a chair, but I don't sit. Good speakers stand.

Dawson looks at the clock on the wall. "Ten minutes, Evvie. I'm serious."

"You got it." I give him a nod. Then I look at Beth again. "First, please be sure you don't let Vandal McDaniel speak at graduation. On Friday, he lit Gus Gus Snyder on fire. Gus Gus was minding his business, reading a book on a bus bench, and Vandal created a fireball in his lap."

"How could a person do that?" Beth's alarm is

palpable, and the other two school board members have the decency to look concerned.

"You light a rag on fire, throw it on something, then douse it with lighter fluid from a squirt gun. Evidently, it's a big sport in some places." Mr. Google told me so.

It's clear I missed Beth's point. "I appreciate the technical description, but my question was how does someone think it's okay to light someone else on fire?"

"Oh." I pause. "You'd have to ask Vandal. Kids like Gus Gus are pretty easy to pick on."

She thinks. "Is Gus Gus a friend of Rose's? His name is familiar."

"Yes. They...hang around the same people." I don't want to talk about the Lair in front of the superintendent.

Dawson speaks up. "Remember, Evvie, you don't know that Gus Gus's assailant was Vandal."

"You're right. I don't. But I saw three identical pickups in Vandal's driveway later that night—and they looked just like the one the firebomb came from." I skip the part about more red trucks at the grocery store. "It would have been easy for him to borrow a truck registered to his dad's farm."

"You don't have the plate number?"

"I would have told you Friday if I did." I give him a crabby look. "Even if Vandal is under suspicion for this

279

crime, that should be enough to keep him from speaking at graduation."

The dude I don't know shakes his head. "In America, you're innocent until proven guilty." The woman I don't know keeps shifting her eyes back and forth among all of us.

"Not if you're Black, Latinx, Asian, Indigenous, or any number of other identities that don't fit the system. Good thing Vandal is white, I guess." I spit it back at him. Rose's mom tries to hide her smile.

Dawson rolls his eyes. "Evvie, we appreciate your thoughts about Vandal. We're discussing it right now."

"Is that why the police officer is here?" I point toward the door. "Does someone have evidence for him?"

Dawson gives me a look that says *Can you please shut your piehole.* "That's all I'm saying right now, Evvie." He looks at the clock. "You have four minutes left. What's the other academic issue?"

I check my camouflage again and take a deep breath. "Mrs. Dearborn says I can't graduate because I'm two points away from a passing grade. Today, my group won a game we played in class, and she normally gives bonus points to the winners of that game, which was my group, but today she didn't. She told me I couldn't do any makeup homework, either. I've turned in all my assignments, and, as you remember, I did most of my sophomore year when I came back as a junior. This was the only class I had left to make up. I also did two presentations that fit the requirements for her class, but she only graded one, and it wasn't the best one. Her decision not to pass me is based on her dislike of me, not on any sound academic principle."

The woman I don't know looks very serious after I say "sound academic principle."

Beth is considering something. "Is she inflexible and rude to others?"

"Not generally, but to me, yes. She's sure I'm a troublemaker when I'm just outspoken. As you might know, those two things are not the same."

"You sure about that?" Rando Dude is clearly not on my side.

Beth reaches out and touches my hand. "You had a hard sophomore year. Things have been all right since you came back?"

I nod. "I've done everything everyone's asked of me, including being the only senior in a sophomore biology class. My foxes presentation, the one she assigned me, wasn't as good as my professional octopus one, but I don't deserve to be kept from graduating."

"You sure about that?" The dude isn't giving up. I give him a look.

Dawson is listening. "How long have you and she been struggling?"

"Since middle school. I called her out when she let kids suffer, and she didn't like it."

The woman I don't know nods at Dawson. "This isn't the first time I've heard about her treatment of kids."

"A few weeks ago, Dearborn saw Vandal pull off Sagal's hijab and didn't do anything." I cross my arms. "What kind of teacher does that?"

The guy I don't know rolls his eyes. "Kids are gonna be kids."

"So you've also taught your children to be bullies?" I've had enough.

"Evvie. Thank you." Dawson stands up. Guess I'm supposed to go.

"Keeping me from graduating by withholding two points seems very cruel. I hope you can grasp that." I look at each one of them. The woman I don't know is nodding. Beth is nodding. Rando Dude is glaring. I glare back.

Dawson takes my elbow and moves me toward the door. "Thank you, Evvie, for your input."

"Thank you, sir, for letting me speak with you all." And I leave.

The cop stands up when I shut the door.

"Are you going to arrest me now? Is that why you were waiting?" It seems plausible, given how many adults have had enough of me.

"Um. No?" He's confused. "I was told to come to the

school and wait in the office for a text. I guess now there's evidence in the parking lot?" He walks out the door, and I follow behind him.

"Evelyn Chambers, go to class!" Marta yells one last time before I'm out of earshot.

The cop is pushing his way out the doors toward the front parking lot. There's a red truck out there, parked so the passenger side door is toward the building. And it has writing on it—big, loopy letters.

He starts to stride faster, not noticing I'm right behind him.

When I get close enough to read what the truck says, I'm ecstatic.

On the hood, it says THIS TRUCK IS THE ONE, in poofy, loopy white letters.

On the passenger door, it says TEST THIS DOOR, PLEASE. Same letters. Lower on the door, in what looks like white paint, it says LIGHTER FLUID RESIDUE ON INSIDE OF DOOR. LEAKY SQUIRT GUN.

On the windshield, there's a capital M with a circle around it.

The cop is too busy walking around the truck to say anything to me. But Dawson's come out the door behind me and is definitely not too busy. "EVVIE CHAMBERS, GET YOUR BUTT TO CLASS."

Lucky for him, I'm done taking photos.

"I'm going, I'm going." I give him a huge, toothy smile as I walk by.

"You're lucky I know you're a good kid." He growls it, almost too quietly for me to hear him.

"I want to graduate, Mr. Dawson." And I walk into school and go to art.

T doesn't even ask me for a pass. I turned in my Aretha drawing yesterday, and they were so pleased with it, they hugged me. Each arm got a particular style, as did Aretha's head—Cubism, Fauvism, Futurism, Modernism, Baroque, Impressionism, Surrealism, Dadaism, and Abstract Impressionism—and my favorite was her arm that said *This is not an octopus arm* in French. T laughed a lot, then told me I could do what I wanted for the rest of the semester. So I sit under the table with my earbuds in.

I send the photos to Rachel: Who got the truck here??? Amazingly, she answers right away.

RACHEL: Carl the Custodian's nephew
Phil works for Vandal's dad on the farm.
He found the truck that smelled like
lighter fluid. The writing is in shaving
cream, so it will eat the paint. The truck
will be marked until Vandal's dad has it
repainted. The Mutiny cares for its own.

EVVIE: 🫤 But why was the cop at school?

RACHEL: 😆😆😆 He's an old classmate of Phil's. Phil told him evidence in Gus Gus's case would be delivered to the school this morning. Once the truck was here, Phil called the police station and the station texted the officer. You were just in the right place at the right time to see it all go down. Vandal's girlfriend—ex-girlfriend by now?—is the real MVP. She felt horrible and went to the cops, so they were sure it was Vandal. Ross drove so Vandal could throw the fire and squirt the lighter fluid. Girlfriend told the cop, the cop told Phil, Phil looked for the truck, and then it all connected.

EVVIE: 🥺 Vandal has a girlfriend? At least she has a conscience.

RACHEL: 😍 Misha Marx, who used to live next door to Gus Gus, I think, before his dad made all that cash. Small towns are sometimes okay.

I send her so many hearts. For you and Gus Gus and Misha.

RACHEL: 🤗 Have you worked on
Dearborn? Played nice?

           EVVIE: 😤 Rejected. I busted in
           on Dawson and the school board
           meeting and told them.

RACHEL: 😆😆😆😆😆😆😆
Good work.

           EVVIE: Thank you.

All of a sudden, I'm exhausted.

           EVVIE: Gonna take a nap under
           T's table.

RACHEL: Good idea. ♥♥♥♥♥♥

I close my eyes. I feel okay, for the first time in four days.
I said what I said.
I don't know if people listened.
But I said it.

Respect existence or expect resistance.
    The stakes are too high to shut up.

25

KEN TEXTS BEFORE SCHOOL.

> **FILM DIVA:** evvie. please. can we talk?
> the mess that is high school is almost
> over. i stopped drinking. i miss you. we
> destroyed our text streak!

I don't reply.
Noon: will you please say something?
I send a cactus emoji, the tall one with the arms.
I can't really conceptualize how I feel. Prickly is close.

Thursday is zoo time. Blue time. I've missed him.

He's been texting for the last week, of course, but I've been brief, though I gave him the general outline of Gus Gus and Dearborn. I don't think he's impressed with my silence.

I walk by the ray pool, and he's on the far side, stroking a ray that's wiggling around so Blue can scratch it in just the right place.

"Hey!" I wave like a Muppet because I'm weird.

He looks up. When he registers it's me, he shows me the swear finger.

"What the hell, mister?"

"One-word texts? Or no texts? From you and your motor mouth?" He's got one hand on the ray and the other in the air, still flying the swear finger.

"I don't talk that much, and it's been some stressful shit, dude!" A woman strolling by with her walker gives me a crotchety look, so I lower my voice as I move toward him. "One of my buddies got set on fire, and I'm not graduating, so it's a wacky time. I'm sorry." When I get to him, I give him a big hug, and he lowers his bird to hug me back. It's so good to be held.

He whispers in my ear. "I was worried about you."

I squeeze him harder. "I'm sorry. It's been wild."

"I know. You told me. I'm being difficult. I'm good at being difficult."

"You are not."

"Maybe you should tell my folks that fact." He squeezes me close before he lets me go, then he reaches down to scratch the ray again, who hasn't left, because obviously it wasn't done being loved.

"Difficulty is fair if people are being jerks. Even parents. Respect existence or expect resistance." I squeeze his hand.

"Nice idea, but Jeff and Michelle don't buy that kind of easy talk."

"I can loan you my mom for a while, if you want— she's the one who taught it to me."

"But if I borrow your mom, wouldn't that make us siblings? We don't want that complication." He gives the ray one more scratch, then a pat. "Go be with your homies." The ray skates away, and Blue picks up the chum bucket. "Are you on your way to see Aretha?"

"Lucie's already texted me photos of the dishes I have to wash today, plus a big spot of mold on the wall that needs treating. But I'm hoping I'll get some cuddle time with her."

"Has Dearborn given up her vendetta yet?"

"What do you think? Teachers are always right."

"I forgot." He takes my hand with the one that's not holding the chum bucket. "Let's go find your girl."

Lucie's got bleach all ready for me, and she points me to the wall with the mold. "Here you go, Evvie! Then I'll show you Aretha's new enrichment."

"Bleach first?" I frown.

"Bleach first." She nods. "It won't take you long."

I scrub walls and dishes, listening to the hum of the tanks and a podcast about octopus behavior. I have no idea where Blue went.

I'm done in twenty-seven minutes. Then I present myself to Lucie. "Okay, boss. I'm done."

"Let's go show Aretha her new challenge." Lucie leads the way to Aretha's corner, and I put my hand in. Aretha is there in a flash, sending two of her arms up mine. Lucie's loading up the new toy with really tiny shrimp, not the normal-sized ones Aretha usually eats.

"Have you had some long days? Me too, honey—me too. Thank you for the cuddles, sweet girl." She's gripping and loosening her arms on me. I pet, very gently, the top of one of her arms above the waterline. She doesn't move it away.

"Here we go, sassy girl." Lucie slips a rectangle made of clear PVC pipe into the tank, a rectangle bigger than Aretha, and I'm forgotten in a flash. Aretha's examining the toy with all of her arms at once, turning it over and over, looking for her task.

"What does she have to do?"

Lucie's watching her like a proud mom. "She's got to extend her arm just right to reach the shrimp. It's easier if she gets in the tube. We'll see how she solves it."

Sure enough, Aretha extends her arms through the

tubes, but she can't quite get the slots open for the shrimp. She gets in the tube, and bam, it's a lot easier—no more reaching—and she has the shrimp out of each corner within ten minutes. Once she's got all the shrimp out, she presents the rectangle to us, resting it against the tank bottom right under where we're standing, as if to say, *What's next? This was too easy.*

"All right, my salty goddess." Lucie's cooing. "I'll see what I can find for tomorrow."

A door bangs open somewhere, and I hear feet. "LUCIE! EVVIE!" It's Blue.

"We're with Aretha," I call back.

He's there in a flash. "I got it! I got the job! I got the JOB!" He's so excited, he starts dancing in a tiny circle, shaking his hips with his arms over his head. Then he runs over and hugs Lucie, who is clapping and cheering him on.

"What job?" My brain is an absolute blank. But as soon as I say it, I realize what he meant. Adventure pals. He's going to Maui.

He's stopped his move toward me and is standing stock-still, blinking. His arms are still out for an embrace. "You don't remember?"

"I do! Of course I . . ."

I see the tears in his eyes, and he starts to back up. "Maui. I'm going to the Maui Ocean Center."

"Of course! I'm so excited for you!" I move toward him, but he backs away and puts his hands up. Out of the corner of my eye, I see Lucie looking between us, trying to sort this out.

"So. You forgot the most important thing in my life right now." He's smiling, but it's not real. "What truly matters to you?"

"I didn't forget, I just blanked! That's different." I'm almost in tears. "I'm so sorry, Blue. It's different!"

His eyes are cold. "It's not different." He stares at me, a mix of shock, sadness, and anger cascading over his face. "How can I compete with everything in your head?" Then he turns and walks out. Without another word.

I don't know what to do.

Lucie looks at me. "He didn't tell you? He applied for a yearlong job at the Maui Ocean Center, where I did research. I wrote him a letter of rec."

I try not to panic. "The place he's visited with his family. Always been his goal for his gap year. With my crazy week, I blanked. Oh my god."

Lucie can see I'm panicking. "Maybe you should go after him?"

"Yes, please."

She shoos me to the door. "Keep me posted."

I run. But I can't find him. And I don't see his Jeep in the parking lot.

OCTO GIRL: blue! it was just a blank moment. i didn't mean anything by it. truly, i'm excited for you! your best adventure is on its way!

I make myself wait three minutes for a reply. No answer.

I go back inside, get my stuff, say goodbye to Lucie, who can tell I'm trying not to sob, and drive home.

OCTO GIRL: you know I didn't mean a single thing by it. my brain is glitchy on its best days, and its not had a good day for a while.

Bubbles.

PELAGIC BLUE: if you cared, you'd remember. let's just be quiet for a while.

My face is hot, like he slapped me.

I sit in my living room. All brain function goes out the window.

Mom is at a meeting, and I can't get my ass out of the chair to feed Popcorn, or myself. Not until it's 9:00 p.m. and the cat is yowling. Mom comes home to a dark house again.

I eat a Pop-Tart and go to bed.

About three, I sit straight up in bed, almost panting.

My heart is pounding. Must have been a bad dream.

I find my phone and text Blue. i am truly, truly sorry that i forgot—momentarily—about Maui and your upcoming adventure. i know it felt very hurtful. if you want to shame me for my brain, then let's not hang out, no matter how cool you are. maybe you have your own shame to work out. and yes, you're cool, in a dorky, oceanic way. i wish you the best, and i hope Maui is amazing. again, i'm sorry.

Fuck shame. Fuck not owning yourself.

Also? Everyone forgets stuff, especially when they're stressed. Not just people with galaxy brains.

It still takes me a long time to go back to sleep.

Blue was pretty wonderful.

Waking up isn't my thing on a good day, but especially not after a hard night. My mom makes me eggs and toast. She can see something's wrong, but she doesn't ask.

The day is a blur. I'm present in all my classes, but I say nothing to no one.

The Lair is popping when I open the door at lunch. Two girls I don't know are sitting on the couch, and Sam's in Gus Gus's spot in the armchair. Sagal's in the other chair. The reset pods are full, and there are two clusters of other kids sitting on the floor. Rose and another girl in her class are planning how to turn more empty cupboards into reset pods. Everyone's chilling and enjoying the vibe. The sign about keys is still on the door to the hallway.

I'd bet money not all of them are neurodivergent.

But if they want to hang with the interesting kids, can I blame them?

After school, I decide it's time to try Popcorn's new leash. I ordered it right after Christmas, but Popcorn yowled so loudly when I took her out in the cold that I stopped trying. Now that it's nice outside, maybe it will go better.

It doesn't. Popcorn hides underneath the bush next to the front steps.

"Same, kitty cat. Same. Stakes are high out here."

I leave her there, wrap the end of the leash around my arm, and sit down to contemplate summer school. I'll have to tell Sarah and Lucie so we can work out the schedule. Then I Google "how to travel the world for free," just in case the aquarium gig doesn't work out. Turns out I can be a soldier or an au pair. I'm not sure either are good solutions.

Mom comes home and follows the leash with her eyes. "Kitty not a nature fan?"

"Not so much."

She holds out her hand to pull me up to standing, and I fish Popcorn out of the bush. She's shaking. Mom hugs us both, and we go inside to make spaghetti.

Popcorn cleans up the parmesan cheese that jumped onto the floor from the grater while the humans sit and eat. We talk about summer. Mom is tutoring kids who will be third-grader busy-brains and working on her thesis, which is about those little busy-brains, so she's got plenty to do.

"You need to get organized with the zoo, whether you graduate or not." My mom points her fork at me before she stands up to put the milk away.

"I know." I take a huge bite and chew. "Talking to Sarah and Lucie is on my list."

"Well, at least you have a list. That's good. I do have a specific piece of news about graduation for you. She pauses and then says, "I hope you're not mad that I investigated it."

I am immediately suspicious. "What did you do?"

She clears her throat, not sure what I'm going to say. "I talked with Bob Dawson today, and he says you can walk in graduation, even with summer school to finish. So you're walking." She's looking directly into my eyes.

"You put everything back together after your sophomore year, and you finished every single thing. It's not your fault this is happening. You are going to celebrate your accomplishment." I see the tears in her eyes. "Got it?"

"Got it." I bring my dishes to the dishwasher.

The relief cascades over her face. "You're not going to fight me?"

"That stupid school owes me a graduation ceremony, even if Dearborn's last two points are keeping me from the actual piece of paper. I should still get presents and cake."

She hugs me again, hands full of leftovers. "Thanks for being willing."

"Fuck Audrey Dearborn." I say it in her ear.

"Indeed." She says it, very clearly, in return.

I want to text Blue. I have to hide my phone so I won't.

I think about texting Ken, but I don't. But I want to. So badly.

I forgot Blue's most important goal. My neglect made my friend so lonely, she drank herself into addiction, maybe.

I go outside, put my bare feet on the grass, and pray for the ground to swallow me up.

26

SATURDAY. KEN GRADUATES. SHE SENDS ME A PHOTO OF HERSELF IN HER gown.

> **FILM DIVA:** i did it! Chicago, here i come! 😊😊😊
>
> <3 <3 <3: 🎁🧁
>
> **FILM DIVA:** want to come over for cake?

I have to sit on my hands to stop myself from replying, because I miss her so much.

Anger, shame, sadness, anger, shame—I am an emotionally frozen pretzel.

Why should any human be able to generate this many tears?

Blue graduates on Sunday. I don't know anyone but him at his school, but I go anyway, and text him a photo of him crossing the stage, and then a photo of his gift, which it took me half an hour to wrap because I suck so much at wrapping gifts. I didn't think to buy a gift bag. It's a Hawaiian shirt.

> **OCTO GIRL:** i know you said not to text, but graduation is special, right? Congratulations!

Nothing.

On the two days between Blue's graduation and my not-graduation, I make lists, play with Popcorn, hide out in the Lair, contemplate melting my Lair key into a lump, turn in my books, give Mrs. Shapiro a flower I picked from someone else's yard, visit Gus Gus, wonder if you can do marine research in the Navy, resist texting Ken, and do anything and everything I can not to think about Blue's silence.

Late Tuesday afternoon. My mom's driving us to the football stadium when my phone vibrates.

PELAGIC BLUE: hey. i suck. i know.

> **OCTO GIRL:** on my way to not
> graduate. later.

Maybe that was rude, but this is not the time.

Like she's read my mind, my mom puts her hand over mine. "You know you don't suck, right?"

"The K–12 school system in the United States would beg to differ." I squeeze her hand and let it go.

"Do not listen to your brain on this one, Evelyn Josephine Chambers. I will not let you." She's put her hands back at ten and two, but now she's got the steering wheel in a death grip. "You aren't allowed to take this personally."

"Explain to me how I can't." I try not to shout. "Dearborn made the calculated decision to flunk me. That's personal. I hurt Blue by not remembering his new job. That's personal. Ken chose not to come to my presentation. That's personal."

"Okay, yes, but what Dearborn did is on her. Not you."

I don't say anything.

"You can't forget that, Evvie. Her abuse of power has everything to do with her own insecurities."

I run this idea through the shredder that's my mind—and I do mean it's a shredder today. Everything has been dumped into its metal jaws, and the teeth are chewing hard and fast. It almost hurts.

"I'm not going to let this go until you understand what I'm saying. I've been studying this stuff for two years, and I've lived it, besides. In school or out, the best thing I ever did for myself was not take other people's rejections personally, especially ones related to my brain." Her knuckles are white, and there's a force underneath her calm that's pretty intense. "You're going to have to answer me with your voice."

"It's so much easier to think you can control it—you know? There must be one more thing I can do, one more thing I can say. Something that will finally make her like me."

Mom laughs, but it sounds kind of like a sob. "There isn't. That's in her control. All you have is you. Controlling shit is a game that creates dopamine, so our brain likes the challenge—but there's just no way." She sounds so sad.

"Remember, I'm not mad at you for this brain."

Another laugh-sob. "I'm mad at myself, so that's mine to sort out, but are we good on the Dearborn thing?"

"We're good."

Her hands relax on the steering wheel. "Excellent. Now get out there and graduate." She's got a real smile on now as she pulls up next to the Gus Gus Bench. The Kid on Fire Bench.

"I'll look for you in the stands." I smile at her and try to back my ass out the door so I don't have to see the crime scene.

"Maybe get out of the car in a regular way?"

"See you later, Mom." I shut the car door and wave, then keep my back to the bench and walk sideways until I can turn toward the school and not see it.

Anybody who saw me thinks I'm even weirder now than they previously assumed.

When I get to the gym, I'm shuffled off to the side for a cap and gown. In our town, they're strictly black, one size, flimsy and slick, but at least you look like you've accomplished something. Even though I haven't. I take a couple photos with a few people—Gus Gus being top of the list, with his bandages. His mom and dad are beaming. Rose takes a selfie with me, and Beth is there, too, though she has to go to the stage since she's on the school board.

Beth hugs me tight. "I'm so sorry. Dearborn's been doing that crap for a long, long time, and she needs to be stopped."

I just hug her back.

She grins when she pulls away. "See you onstage." She puts her arm around Rose, and they both walk off.

Sam wanders up, snapping candids with the school's nice Digital Journalism camera. "Smile, Evvie!"

I stick my tongue out. "Who let you have that?"

"Rachel." He points. "I'm not sure who told her she could have the camera." He walks away, snapping and pointing at people. They oblige him with pure goofiness.

"Evvie!" I hear Rachel's voice behind me, and I turn around.

She envelops me before I have a second to think about it. "I'm so glad you came. Your mom told me she was going to try to talk you into it."

I break away from her because her hug is intense. "This place owes me, and I want cake. I'll figure out the two fucking points this summer."

"That's the spirit!" She kisses me on the cheek and runs off to hug and kiss someone else.

All of a sudden, I'm so tired, I need to sit down. I collapse on top of a rolled-up wrestling mat.

This place almost killed me. Then it refused me.

And I'm still here.

Everyone's happiness and excitement swirls around me, and I don't move. I might be dead.

I hear a loud voice. "Let's go, students. Line up alphabetically!" It's Garfield, by the gym doors, with a bullhorn.

I've stood between Heath Chamberlain and Katelin Clausen since we were in kindergarten. We nod at one another, and then we're marching off behind Garfield, toward the football field.

The shadows are starting to form, but it's a gorgeous May evening. There are LOTS of people in the stands, plus all the chairs for us on the field—don't the chairs mess their field up?—and we march right in and sit right down. There are maybe seventy-five of us. Vandal is nowhere to be seen, which is exactly as it should be, and neither is Ross. Rumor has it Vandal was arrested and booked on first-degree assault charges, but, of course, his dad bailed him out—though he may have made Vandal sit in jail overnight. I don't believe the second part. I also heard Gus Gus's parents are suing Vandal's family, but that could be another uninformed rumor. If Vandal had shown his face today, I would have punched it.

The band plays "The Star-Spangled Banner," Dawson and Garfield each say something, the choir sings a pointless song, and then it's time for the student speaker. With Vandal out, they went to Gus Gus, and he refused, so it's a girl named Kacey Thorson. She looks like she's going to wet her pants. Nobody can hear her at first, but Dawson gets the mic adjusted, and then it's better. She makes it through with pretty standard inspirational stuff, with the exception of a quotation from Ozzy Osbourne. That makes people laugh. Garfield rolls his eyes so hard, we can see it in the first two rows, and we laugh harder.

Kacey sits down, and Dawson stands up to say the standard "by order of the state of Minnesota" stuff. Then

Marta goes to the podium to read our names, and Dawson, Garfield, the school board guy I don't know, and Beth line up to shake our hands as we get our diploma covers.

I'm the twelfth kid in our class, so I get to the bottom of the steps pretty quickly.

"Evelyn Josephine Chambers." Marta says it just like I didn't bust into that school board meeting, like she didn't get snippy when I told her to call Gus Gus's mom, like she hasn't glared at me every time I've been in the office. It's the second time someone's said my full name today.

I walk up the stairs and across the stage, smiling as big as I can, and I hear cheering from the far side, up at the top of the stands. My mom is waving her hands and clapping, and so is Sarah, right along with Lucie. And Blue. Blue is here. Sitting next to Blue is Ken. Fucking hell.

Focus, Evvie.

I stick my hand out to Dawson, who shakes it and says, "Congratulations, Evvie. I'm proud of you." He's got a real smile on his face, not a fake one, and it surprises me.

"Well—"

"Keep walking." He says it through his smile, and I keep walking.

I shake Garfield's hand, and he doesn't seem to know me at all. That's fine.

Rando Dude from the school board meeting holds

out his hand, and I shake it hard. "Good luck, firecracker."
He sneers when he says it, but just for a second.

"Good luck not being a jerk." Whoops. Then I'm on
to Beth.

"Again, Evvie, congratulations. Proud of you." She
grips my hand with both of hers and smiles really big.

"Thanks." I smile big, too, because Beth is a good
human, and go back to my seat.

Everyone who went ahead of me is looking in their
folder, even though nothing's in there. But you just gotta
check, you know?

I open mine, and there's a folded piece of paper.

What more can they do to me?

Evvie:

*Remember when Sam mooned Dearborn
because of what she said to Rose? A girl in my
class flipped Dearborn off after Dearborn made
fun of me, and she spent two days in the Hole.
I baked her cookies.*

*Dearborn's been doing this stuff for
twenty-five years, if not longer.*

*I told Mr. Dawson my story, and I
threatened to take it public that she withheld
your two points—and then your five bonus
points! He wasn't interested in the publicity.*

He asked other teachers for stories, which
they gave him, and then he went to Dearborn.
Her choice was a formal reprimand and
a conversation with a reporter from the
Bluestem Lake Tribune, in my presence, or
passing you in Biology. She chose to give you the
points.

> *Mr. Dawson told me I could write you this*
> *note. Rose is so glad you use your voice. She*
> *looks up to you.*

> *Happy graduation! No summer school!*
Sending a big hug,
Beth

My mouth is hanging open. I can feel it.

I look up on the stage, and Beth is in between students. She gives me a big thumbs-up and wipes her eyes. I give her a thumbs-up in return and wish I had some Kleenex. The tears just get smeared around with the sleeve of my plastic gown.

There's a tap on my shoulder. I turn around, and it's Aurora Hansen with a wad of Kleenex. Aurora was my bestie in first grade. "Graduation's just an emotional time, isn't it?"

"On so many levels. Thank you." And then I get myself together.

EMOTIONS IN MY BRAIN

1. relief
2. relief
3. relief
4. relief
5. relief
6. relief
7. love
8. a tiny portion of calm joy

Of course I lose it again when Gus Gus goes across the stage, and then I can't stop the tears. The choir stands up to sing another song, and I sob my way through that, trying to be quiet and just let the tears happen, but my body disagrees, so I end up hiccupping, which raises the embarrassment level. Heath puts his hand on my shoulder, and Katelin takes my hand, and we listen to the choir while I cry.

We're classmates, not even friends. But they steady me—random, weird me. Then the hiccups get manageable, and the tears are stopping, and we're standing up and marching out, and it's OVER.

High school is over. And I fought back.

Once we all make it to the empty end of the football field, we're clapping and cheering, and other people besides me are crying. Gus Gus can't open his mouth very widely, but he's still yelling "yaaaaaay!" and doing his best jazz hands, and Misha, Vandal's ex-girlfriend and Gus Gus's ex-neighbor, is standing right next to him. You can see how red the palms of Gus Gus's hands still are, which stabs me in the heart. He looks happy. Dude is still going to MIT. And Vandal went to jail, at least for a little bit.

Everyone starts to disperse in the growing darkness, looking for their parents and families, and I start searching for my mom. But the first people I see are Sarah and Lucie, walking toward me with huge grins and a gift bag.

"We're so proud, Evvie!" "So proud!" "We'll help you with summer school." "We can help you study." "Aretha is proud, too!" They're both talking at once, and I hug them.

"We can't wait for you to see this!" Lucie shoves the gift bag at me. "Open it now!"

I do, and it's the coolest octopus T-shirt I've ever seen, plus there's a photo in a frame. It's me, cooing into the tank, and you can see a couple of Aretha's arms winding themselves up my arm.

"You and your sea goddess." Sarah's got tears in her eyes. "She's ready to have you around every day."

I hug her again.

There's a tap on my shoulder, and I turn around. Blue's standing there with a cake, looking shy and awkward, but adorable. Ken's right next to him.

I don't know which one to talk to first.

Blue holds out the cake. "Happy graduation. Please don't be mad. I overreacted. Freaky brain and all that."

I look at Ken. "Thanks for coming. Please don't be mad. I've wanted to text you so many times. I overreacted. Freaky brain and all that."

Pause. Then the three of us rush each other for a big hug, with a cake in the middle. I cry a little bit more, but they don't hold that against me.

"I'm sorry, Evvie." Blue kisses me on the cheek.

"I'm sorry, Ken." I kiss Ken on the cheek. "I'm sorry, Blue." I kiss him on the cheek.

"You dorks are the goofiest people I know, but that's why you're the best." Ken kisses both of us on the cheek. "Can we have cake now?"

"Obviously the two of you have met." I take the cake from Blue. "What kind is it?"

"Your favorite, of course." He looks proud of himself.

"How do you know what my favorite cake is?"

He shrugs. "You told me. Carrot cake, without raisins, but with cream cheese frosting."

The top of the cake says EVVIE THINKS HIGH SCHOOL IS DUMB. "The sentiment is spot-on."

Finally, my mom gets there, because she's been talking to people. I saw her give Beth a hug. Mom looks like she's been crying, even though she wouldn't want me to see that.

I pounce on her. "Did you know I was gonna graduate for real? And how did you know who Blue was?"

Blue's eyes get wide. "You graduated?"

I nod.

Ken's mouth is hanging open. "You weren't gonna graduate?"

"Nope. Dearborn's a bitch. Long story."

"That's really low." Ken's face gets stormy. "And you gotta tell me these things."

"I was mad at you."

She lowers her eyes. "Sober since that day."

I hug her again, once I pass the cake back to Blue. "Good."

Then I realize I derailed my train of thought. "Back to you, Mom. Did you know what Beth did? And how did you find Blue?"

Her smile is watery. "I knew what Beth was trying to do. I didn't know if she'd succeed. And you posted a photo from Zoo Prom on Instagram."

"Good thing I did that. So you wanted me here, just in case. And you were ready to fight me."

"But then"—she spreads her arms really big—"you came here willingly! Who knew you would, in fact, do something I asked you to do?"

Everyone laughs. Me too.

Then the tiredness comes back, and I feel like I'm gonna

fall down. "Could we, um, go home and eat this cake? I don't have anything to be tense about, so my body's kind of boneless." I start to slump, just to see what happens.

Ken takes one arm, and Lucie takes the other. They steer me to the parking lot, with Blue, Sarah, and Mom behind us. We go to our house and eat cake on the lawn after Mom goes to get gas station pizza. I eat some cake with my hands, because I can.

It's my graduation day.

I kicked the ass of high school.

I outsmarted it.

I outlasted it.

Everyone's long gone when Blue and I move to the backyard to check out the stars. It's the first time he's been to my house. We get a blanket and lie down on the grass. Spring is the greatest season ever.

He picks up my hand. "I leave for Maui in two weeks. I'll bring Fishee Stixx over the day before my flight."

"I'll warn Popcorn." I squeeze his hand. "That's really soon. But there's FaceTime. You're gonna want to see Fishee, for sure."

"Maybe you could come visit? Not just through my phone? Maybe we could be adventure buddies in person. Quest pals." He doesn't look at me, just at the dark sky with its glitter. "Small towns have less light pollution."

"Maybe. And yeah. Less light pollution." I'm not thinking about light pollution when I roll over to look at him. "Maybe we could make the most of these two weeks?" And I kiss him. For a long time.

Then we're just sharing the blanket again.

"I'm sorry, Evvie. I was mean about your brain."

"I'm sorry I forgot about something so important to you."

We stay outside for a long, long time.

When I wake up—very, very, very late on Wednesday morning—I find a message from Rachel: gotta bring your key back. ☹️☹️☹️☹️☹️☹️☹️☹️☹️☹️☹️☹️☹️☹️☹️☹️

> **EVVIE:** You CANNOT let them shut down the Lair. Kids need that space. They need you! They need peace.
>
> **RACHEL:** ☹️☹️☹️ I'm trying.

BLAHS lets out at 3:08. At 3:15, I use my Lair key one last time. Everyone else has seven more school days, so I'm sure Rachel won't let them touch the Lair until school's done for the year.

Can an average, ordinary place be magic?

Depends on who's in the space, I think.

I knock on Rachel's office door, then open it. She's

typing but looks up when she sees me and cocks her head at a chair. I sit.

She finishes whatever she was typing, then extends her hand, palm up. "Got your key?"

I hold it up.

She flips her hand upright for a high five, so I slap her one. "Turn it into a necklace. Do whatever you want." She pulls a handful of keys just like mine out of her drawer.

"Huh?"

She smiles. "I made copies of mine for Garfield and will give them to him in"—she looks at the clock—"twelve minutes. So you can keep yours. And we've already got the okay to keep the Lair open. Garfield's threat is defeated."

"What?" She's going too fast.

She points at me. "Your words preserved the Lair for Rose, Sam, Sagal, and whoever else will need it."

"They did?"

She nods. "And besides that, we have a new member of the Mutiny, sworn to secrecy just like all the rest of us." She studies my confusion. "Do you get me?"

"Nope."

She's exasperated. "Who might have stopped repping for the jocks, preps, and socials? Your exact words, which he'll probably remember for a long time. He told me he wanted to come in clutch for the weirdos and the regular kids."

BOOM.

"Dawson saved the Lair?"

She comes around her desk and hugs me. "He told me he's going to put Garfield off, then install a keypad lock on the door. I get to say who has the code, in consultation with other teachers, but those students can let other ones in, if they want. And guess what I'm going to make the code?" Big grin.

"I have no idea." This conversation is knocking me out.

"Nine two six four."

"Why?"

"If you have letters on your keypad, it spells out WANG." She hugs me again. "I'm proud of you for speaking up. Now scram. I've got to get my camouflage on for Garfield." She starts scooping the keys into her hands and transferring them to her pocket. "We'll hang out this summer, since I'm not your teacher anymore. That work for you?"

"Absolutely."

"Did you know your mom and I went to high school together? She's a few years older than me."

BOOM. Again. "This last five minutes has blown my mind to smithereens."

She laughs. "Go enjoy being done with this place."

I leave her office and go stand in the Lair. Then I grab two pieces of paper and a marker.

REASONS TO USE YOUR VOICE

1. *It's yours.*
2. *You have important things to say.*
3. *If people say you talk too much, go somewhere else.*

Then I make five more blank spaces and number them. Other Lair kids will write their own reasons.

EVVIE CHAMBERS'S
RULES FOR CAMOUFLAGE

1. *When you need to. No hesitation. Always protect yourself.*
2. *Find people you're safe with so you don't have to.*

Same thing. Six more numbered blank spaces. I'm not the only expert.

I write really big, for both lists. Then I tack both pieces of paper on the door to the band room.

Then I holler "HOP OFF MY WAAAAAAAA-ANG!" as loud as I can, for at least fifteen seconds, and it's so satisfying. Rewarding to my very core. Then I climb out the window, just for old times' sake, put the screen back, and go home.

27
LAST WORDS

1. Don't
2. let
3. the
4. neurotypicals
5. get
6. you
7. down.
8. Amen.

If you're a friend of Evvie's, I'll talk to you.
Octopuses are **selective**.

You humans think you're considering us.
Studying and judging us.
We're considering you, too.

Here's the truth:
brain differences are part of **normal human variation**.
Maybe 10 percent of humans have different brains. Maybe more.
It's a useful thing. **Helpful**, even.
Innovation comes from variation.
But some people are **threatened** by difference.
It's **dangerous**. Intimidating. Out of order.
Especially if it's sneaky and unpredictable.
Difference should be **ridiculed**.

Bullshit.

Octopuses know "different" is just fine.

I mean, look at me.

Blue blood, three hearts, **nine brains**,

    the ability to escape from almost any

    enclosed space through the tiniest crack,

    and the skin-morphing skill to camouflage

    myself better than any other animal.

My entire body is thinking, feeling, and

    exploring. All the time.

You can tell when I like something.

You see my skin change when I'm frustrated

    or frightened.

Humans call me **amazing**. Unique. Fantastical.

    Unlike any other creature on Earth.

Humans find nature endlessly fascinating.

    You build universities to study the

    variety.

So why do people get upset the instant
a *person* demonstrates some variety?
Humans are different colors, sizes, shapes,
and genders, with different ways to think,
love, dress, and act. **You are beautiful
and exciting.**
Why do you punish the different ones?
A bigger question: **who made the
definitions of "different"?**
Do you need to uphold arbitrary rules?

You could fix it, you know.
So no more Evvies get told they're wrong.
Dumb. Weird. Strange.
No more kids feel shame or sorrow over
their brains.
No more kids hide or keep to themselves.
No more wonder if their "difference" is lovable.

No more become self-conscious, anxious
adults.

What stops you?

**The ones you label "different" are the
most beautiful.**
They think the most interesting thoughts.
They love most thoroughly.
They create the most interesting things.
Let them be their beautiful cephalopod selves.

Are they being difficult? Or are you?

*   *   *

ACKNOWLEDGMENTS

First, thank you to the people who helped me create Evvie and her pals. Thank you to Nolan and Peter Schmit, Mitchell Aiken, Carrie Mesrobian, Amy Sarig King, and my long-ago student RM for helping me understand these young humans. Thank you tons to Rachel Gold for helping me understand myself, so I could write this book. Thank you to the real Mx. Thompson, for beta reading (ha ha, that's a pun) Evvie and providing high school intel. Thank you to Stella Haroldson for reading and liking Evvie, and thank you to Wayne Whitmore for school board advice. Thank you to Nadine Nagata and Tessa at the Maui Ocean Center for allowing me to meet their day octopuses in December 2019—best birthday present ever. Thanks—as always, eternally—to my Siblings in Ink, who read, critique, encourage, and believe;

extra thanks to Rachael for our text adventures. Thanks to Ann Fee for letting me share my Beautiful Brains coloring pages from the Arts Center booth at Rock Bend. Thanks to the Minnesota State Arts Board for the grant that helped this book along, and to South Central College for a sabbatical that allowed me to finish a passable draft. And thanks to Grover, for love and patience while I write, plus thanks to Mother Nature, Lake Superior, the Judson Bottom Road, the prairie and the Great Plains, raptor migration, spring, sunsets, my dog who walks for miles, and my goofball cats, for keeping me grounded and connected.

Then, thank you to the people who created the actual book. Heaps of thanks to Michaela Whatnall, for taking a chance on Evvie, and more heaps of thanks to Margaret Raymo, for choosing Evvie. Thank you to Michael Bourret for advice on earlier drafts. A GIANT thank-you to all the individuals at Little, Brown Books for Young Readers who made this manuscript into a tangible object and then promoted it. I am indebted. Special thanks to the editors, copy editors, and proofreaders who were patient with the format of this book (!). Thank you to Kimberly Glyder for the gorgeous cover art. Thanks to E. Eero Johnson for his illustrations and for our collabs, which are always a joy.

Finally, thank you to the people who form *my* foundation, and thus the foundation of this book. I'm privileged to have so many neurodivergent loved ones (if I try to name you all, I'll forget someone and be horribly embarrassed). Shae David, thanks for teaching me so much. I love you a zillion. Birth, extended, married-into, and chosen family members with unruly brains, same. All other friends and students with rowdy brains, also same. A special thank-you to my neurodivergent students for helping me sharpen my teaching skills to better serve all students. Special shout-out to Cronns everywhere (and the Keeney/Peters pair) for *excellent* conversations, lifelong learning, and knowing the value of curiosity. I was well into my twenties before I found out neurotypicals aren't necessarily fond of our ways—I honestly had no idea. Thanks for being you and supporting me in being myself. I love you.

If I've forgotten anyone, I humbly apologize.